Papers Poetry & Prose volume V

An anthology of eighth grade writing

Students at Pierce Middle School

iUniverse, Inc.
New York   Bloomington

Papers Poetry & Prose volume V
An anthology of eighth grade writing

This is a work of fiction. All of the characters, names, incidents, organizations, and dialogue in this novel are either the products of the author's imagination or are used fictitiously.

iUniverse books may be ordered through booksellers or by contacting:

iUniverse
1663 Liberty Drive
Bloomington, IN 47403
www.iuniverse.com
1-800-Authors (1-800-288-4677)

ISBN: 978-1-4502-5895-1 (sc)
ISBN: 978-1-4502-5896-8 (ebook)

Printed in the United States of America

iUniverse rev. date: 09/07/2010

Gone Forever
By Josh Alicea

His name is Carlos,
He's tall and hilarious,
He's my hero.

He always stood up for me,
But he's more than that,
He's my big brother.

He's my role model,
He's the one brother who never gets in trouble.
He's my idol.

I looked up to everything he did.
But he's more than that,
He's my big brother.

He's always there,
Whenever I pleaded for him,
Always by my side.

Whenever I needed him,
But he's more than that,
He's my big brother.

It's been four years,
and some odd days,
I miss my brother.

And then I realize,
My big brother is
Gone forever.

1

Friendship Means...
By Latasha Allen

Trust
friends wish to have a long relationship and to be friends forever.
Friends fear losing their best friend by something that will happen or what did happen to them.
Friendship is something you can have a longtime even when the person moves somewhere else.
Friend tell each other things that happened to them.

Honesty
Friends wish to have nothing come between them.
Friendship is about no fighting a lot and getting along with each other.
Friends don't lying to each other about things.

Respect
Friends fight about things then still get over it and still have a good relationship.
Friends go places even if they just got in to a fight.

Wonders
Who wonders what it would be like if we weren't friends or if we never met?
Who wonders if we don't talk again?
What if we fight again?
What are we going to do over the weekend?

Excitement
Friends go lots of places and remember all the places they go.
Friends see lots of things together.
Friends lend each other things.

The Accident
By Murphy Allen

Have you ever had one of those days? The kind that start as the best of your life and then changes to the worst possible in the world? Let's just say I had a day that went something like that! It was May or June, I was still in school. I was in 2nd grade and I still had my old bike. The girly kind that was purple and pink and had sparkles on it and a little basket on the front. I had a friend who lived in my neighborhood and I always rode my bike to his house. I was over there on this particular day, the day that I thought I might die.

It was noon when my dad called to tell me to come home for lunch. I said my goodbyes and walked out to the driveway to grab my bike. Now, my friend's driveway is on a steep hill which makes riding down really fun. So instead of walking down like usual, I decided it would be more fun to ride from the top. Big mistake! I climbed on the bike, pushed off the ground, and started pedaling. I was right; it was fun, at least until I noticed something very wrong. I was going fast, way faster than I needed to be. Faster and faster, I started to panic. The hill didn't look as steep as it really was. My legs kept pedaling faster; I couldn't control them I couldn't even think straight. When I thought it couldn't get worse my heart seemed to stop. Right across from the street, right in my path, was a big solid rock. My 2nd grader brain told me to swerve. Now! If I didn't it would be very bad. However my 2nd grader reflexes didn't react in time and time itself seemed to hate me that day. In a split second the front tire hit the rock and sent me flying over the handlebars.

When my brain registered what had happened I was lying on the rock with my bike in a jumbled mess on top of me. Jolts of pain shot through my right cheek though I didn't know why. My knees were scraped from falling on the hard stone. I started sobbing but I didn't even know the worst of it. I looked down and saw small dots of blood on the stone. My cheek was hurting even more than my knees. It felt as if needles were being pounded into my face. I reached up to feel it. My hand hit one of the handlebars on my bike. I pushed it away and returned to touch my cheek. My hand felt warm and wet on my cheek which I thought was strange. My cheek was warmer than usual, a lot warmer. When I took my hand off, it was red. Blood! I was bleeding really badly. I felt a giant hole in the side of my face. Ruby red blood ran down my cheek until it dripped off my chin. It was all over my hand, sliding down my arm. I was terrified now.

My friend's dad saw the whole incident and was rushing into his car. He pulled up beside me and jumped out with a washcloth in his hands. He pried the bike off of me and helped me stand. He helped me into his car and gave me the washcloth he was carrying. It was warm and felt good on my cheek. He drove me to my house. My dad then took me to the doctor's office. When we arrived we were put in one of the patient rooms. A doctor came in and examined my cheek. It wasn't hurting as much now but throbbing instead, like a heart. When he was finished he took out a needle and stuck it into the skin that was still left on my cheek. Probably to numb it down. I flinched when the shot went in but it wasn't half as bad as the pain I had felt recently. The doctor pulled out a sewing needle and some kind of black plastic thread. He made me lay down on the bed and started to sew up my cheek. I saw the needle come towards me and started freaking out, kicking, and trying to get away. I didn't want some stranger to come at me with a needle and even though I was given a numbing shot I still felt some pain. My dad and some other nurses had to hold me down until it was over. It felt like forever until the doctor was done.

In the end it took twelve stitches to sew up the giant hole. Even though the scar left over is small and hard to see, I still remember that terrible feeling when I thought I was going to die.

My Passion
By: Nick Andrews

Under my skin is my heart.
Under my heart is my passion,
my passion is camping.
Hiking under red and orange leaf covered trees,
a pack on my back.
Birds of all colors flying around,
cardinals and sparrows.
Foxes and squirrels running about,
fast and swift.
And seeing all the sights everywhere I go.
Colorful fish swimming in the water,
other sea life doing the same.
Or hiking through the sand dunes,
hot and bright,
but still enjoying the scene.
Under my passion is enjoying life.
Having fun with friends and family,
learning new things.
Walking the trails while playing around,
sharing all the memories collected.
Under all of this is your passion.

Stitches
By Jacob Ashley

One time I went to my friend Noah's house. He had moved from Waterford to Hartland, Michigan. His new house had three stories, a huge yard with a lot of steep rocky hills, and he was still supposed to get a in - ground swimming pool. It was winter time and I was staying over at his house for the night. We got bored of staying inside and we decided to go outside and slide down the hills in his back yard.

It really wasn't a good idea because it was steep, rocky, and had some stuff on it like wire from the previous owner, and to add to that at the very bottom of the hill was a road. So I found the highest and steepest point on his hill that I could find. But when I slid down it and tried walking back up the hill, I realized that my knee was throbbing from pain. So when I got back to the top of the hill Noah and I started going back to his house. But when I was like half way there I decided that it was probably a good idea to see what was wrong with my knee. So I looked down and saw that my snow pants were soaked with my blood. So then Noah ran ahead and got his parents because then we knew that it was probably something serious.

So when I finally got back to his house I sat down on his staircase and his mom took a look at my knee. When we rolled my jeans and snow pants up we saw that I had a deep gash in my leg that I would definitely need stitches for. So Noah's mom called my mom and told her what was going on and my mom came to pick me up and take me to the ER right next to the MJR, cinema 16 movie theater. The doctor gave me a shot that injected a type of medicine in my knee so it wouldn't hurt when he was giving me stitches. I needed like six or seven stitches when I was finally done. My dad had come from work when my mom called him and he arrived in the middle of when I was getting stitches. When I was done my dad had told me that it was so deep that he could see my bone when the doctor was giving me stitches. Noah's dad called about a day later and told my parents that he and Noah went back out to try and find what could have caused the gash in my leg but they couldn't find anything. Today I still have the scar on my knee.

Broken Arm
by: Jessica Bailey

Any time I hurt myself I tell myself, "At least it doesn't hurt as bad as it did when I broke my arm." It was a cold (normal) day in Iceland, I was nine years old in the fourth grade. We were all outside for a freezing recess. There were a bunch of us playing on the soccer field. We decided to play tag. We were all running around and screaming. Some of us decided to take our game out of the field and we went all the way around it. I ran along with three girls and a boy. We were outside the fence, it had two openings to get in and out. After running ourselves silly we were tired. So I tried to convince the kids that we should just go back on the field and they agreed.

As I slid between one of the openings, I saw the person that was it, was coming towards me, and at the same time my friend sol called my name, and because the other person was coming at me I raised my hand "meaning one sec" and as I raised my right arm and I hit it really hard on the fence. It all happened so fast I wasn't exactly sure what had happened for a minuet, but I ended up on the ground and as soon as I opened my eyes my friend sol was right next to me. She asked if I was ok, and I told her I was fine and that my right arm felt like it was going to blow up. Then she told me to get up before one of the kids run over you, and as I used my arm to get up I fell back down and had the worst feeling in my arm, and I was screaming so loud that the people on the field all came running over, and out of nowhere the gym teacher and the assistant principle came running and they asked my what was wrong and I just kept screaming saying " MY ARM, MY ARM!!" and then I took off my sweater and the bone in my arm was sticking out and when I saw it, I started to cry even more, not sure why but I did.

Later the gym teacher and that asst. principal began to argue whether or not to call the ambulance…they finally decided to just call my mom, it seemed like it took forever for my mom to get there, but she finally did. As soon as we got to the emergency room there were doctors there that put me in a wheelchair and took me to the ex-ray room, I asked if my mom could come but he told me that it was only going to take a minuet, and it did. When I came out my mom wasn't outside the door, but then he took me down the hall and she was in the waiting room on the phone, I wondered who it was, but didn't bother to ask. We started walking down another hall, and I could hear somebody screaming, but the further down the hall I went the screaming slowly disappeared.

The first thing we did when we got into the room was that he lifted me up and put me on the bed that was in the room, then he started stirring some kind of tan-yellowy color that had steam coming out of it, then he got a bandage and cut them and laid them down on the table, a few minuets later a nurse came in with the ex-rays and put them on a board had had light on the back of it. He started to look and said that it was broken, and that it could have been a lot worse! Then he told me that they have to get me some pain medication in me so that I couldn't feel them, putting the bone back in place. The pain medication didn't seem to work. It hurt so badly, that I thought about how much more it would have hurt with out the medication in, OUCH! The way that they fixed it was that they stuck 2 needles and moved the bones to go to normal place that it was suppose to be. When they stuck the needles in I started screaming so loud that I fainted, and when I woke up I had a cast on, it was super warm under it, and uncomfortable. My mom was in the room, but I'm not sure she knew I was awake because her back was facing me. I called her and she looked over and said "Oh you're awake".

After this every time I hurt my arm I tell myself, at least it doesn't hurt as bad as it did when I broke my arm. And now my arm is ok, well most of the time, because in gymnastics I cant straighten my arm on the bar. But that's ok because I'm going to switch to tumbaling.

By Joe Baker

Hockey,
Intense, fast,
Hitting, shooting, skating,
Slap shot, showdown,
Ice fun!

Great sport,
Playing begins,
Sliding, icing, striking,
Go to the net!
Stick Puck!

Fights,
Contact, blood,
Falling, crashing, tumbling,
Hockey fun.
Rumble!

Playoffs,
Slam, hits,
Timing, scoring, winning
Race to the puck!
Post-season!

I miss you!
By: Tori Bass

I remember when we were best friends, when we supported each other.

You were always the first person I called. When I found something out you're the first one I told.

I remember when we were there for each other, when I wasn't in a good mood you invited me over, or when my parents were fighting, you talked on the phone with me... all night.

Isn't that amazing how fast things can change?

We started to find new friends which we both weren't ok with. But why didn't either of us make an effort to fix it?

Couldn't you see the pain I was in from losing you?

Couldn't you see the jealousy in my eyes?

Why weren't you fighting for me? Why weren't you trying to talk to me and fix things?

Why wasn't I fighting for you?

I wish I knew how to answer these questions.

My Great Friend
By: Jacob Bearden

In October, one of the greatest people I've ever known, Michael Gaddes, passed away at the age of 27. He was a brother, a son, a husband, and to me a great friend. He was loving, caring, funny, and the strongest person I knew although each day was a struggle. He was one of those people that no matter what the circumstances are, they always put a smile on and gave others one too. He made the most of every day and never took one for granted. Though I didn't get to spend a lot of time with him, the time I did was priceless. He helped me through hard times when I was sick. When he was around he was always concerned and was trying to cheer me up. The time with him that I will remember the most would be when his brother underwent a double lung transplant. While we were waiting for the news he was trying to cheer everyone up and comforting the ones who needed it. He would tell everyone that it would be alright and did things like play cards with the whole family to take our minds off the things that could go wrong. These are just some examples of the many good things he did while he was here.

For his entire life he has battled, Cystic Fibrosis, a disease that attacks the respiratory system. Throughout his life, he did everything he could to deal with it until about two and half years ago it became too much. His condition worsened until he was forced to undergo a double lung transplant about a year later. He eventually began to recover and was able to return home.

About a year and a half after the lung transplant, he suddenly, could not breathe. He was rushed to "The University of Michigan Hospital" and was stabilized. It was decided a couple of weeks later that he would have to be flown to Cleveland to wait for another double lung transplant. Sadly, it was too long for him to wait and his only cling to life was taken away. His heart stopped.

His friends and family were all devastated. The funeral was an emotional event. His procession was the biggest in the "homes" history. It was filled with all who knew and loved him. Although he is gone and missed, he will never be forgotten and will always be in our hearts.

His death had a huge impact on everyone that knew him. It has shown us a new view of life and how we should cherish every day because it could be our last. His life also taught us how to be better friends and family members. He also showed us that you shouldn't look at the "bads" in life, but use your time to appreciate and make the best of what you have.

By Chase Berry

Aggressive Inline
Fun thrilling pleasure
Exiting, activity Xgames skate-parks sponsorship
Challenging doing better sport series adrenaline pumping falling pain
Bruises cuts brakes fractures hospital
New tricks trying harder nationals
Aggressive inline

Hockey
Goals Pro's Fouls
Penalty Players Sticks Net's Red wings
Coaches Team's Stanley cup
Hockey

School
Work boring not fun
7hrs homework pencil paper pen
Teachers classes detentions
School

My Aunt Jenny
By: Taylor Bond

One of my favorite people in the world is my Aunt Jenny. She always made me feel good about myself; whenever I was in a crabby mood she was always the first one to hug me. But four years ago she passed away from breast cancer. Even when she fought breast cancer for five years she always had a smile on her face for her three boys, Nick was her oldest son he was 17 when she passed away, Andrew was her middle child he was 15, her youngest Zach he was only 12. Her sons and her were really close she was a great mom to them; she would always try and do what was best for them. She is the kind of person that would put you first before herself; one time when she was done getting chemotherapy she made time to play games and have fun with everyone

Between her and I she was like my second mom, she would always cheer me up when I was down; she was my biggest role model. She would always take good care of me. I used to see her almost everyday because she used to babysit me. I remember when we would go out on the slip-and –slide and I would always try to do really cool tricks but I would always get hurt, she would give me a hug and say its okay and of course I went back out and tried it again.

When my mom told me that she was sick I thought she would get better, I was only 11 at the time so I thought that the medicine would cure it. I asked my mom everyday if I could see her and she replied the same thing : "I'm sorry honey but she doesn't want anyone to see her like this", after about four months later they still wouldn't let me see her, I knew something bad was going to happen or it already had.

Then one hot summer day on June 6th my dad picked my sister and I up from school early, when I got in the car I was babbling my mouth about an upcoming field trip, then I noticed my dad was looking a little somber. I asked him what was wrong, he let out a deep sigh and said "I'm sorry girls but your aunt jenny passed away this morning." All I remember was that I looked over at my sister of course she was sad but myself, I had tears fill my eyes and I felt in a way, mad. It didn't feel right that the world could go on so perfectly, didn't anyone know that a person I love so much is gone? My aunt jenny has left and I didn't get to say goodbye.

SUMMER
By: Maria Brado

Warmth . . . the spirit of summer.

No School . . . hanging out with your friends everyday.

Grass . . . the soft blanket that cradles your bare feet and tickles your toes.

Late Nights . . . sitting around the campfire and looking up at the stars.

Lemonade . . . the cold, sweet, sour, liquid that quenches your thirst.

Ocean . . . a deep blue bath you soak in.

Sleeping in . . . dreaming your dream.

Summer . . . the warmth, no school, green grass, late nights, sour lemonade, deep blue ocean, and sleeping in of summer.

Taekwondo
By Terril Branner

Taekwondo is hard,
and exhausting.

Learning new moves,
moving up belts
is challenging.
It makes me practice everyday.

Kicking,
punching and moving,
teaching me to protect myself.

Taekwondo

By: Brazzell, Christopher

Once there was a teenager named Zack, he was a great scientist. In his lab, one day, he was working on a very important project. He intended to reach the future with his new machine. He was finally ready to try it and he turned it on. Suddenly the machine exploded! Zack flew back and hit the wall unconscious. Slowly he came to and found little animals climbing on him and sniffing him. With slow movements he scared the animals away. He was stiff for a while and had to stretch out and move around a bit so his body would wake up. He heard something in the bushes behind him, he looked cautiously. Then a large animal jumped out at him and he ran and ran for what seemed like an hour.

After he caught his breath and got himself to safety, he thought it was gone, But all of the sudden he heard a heart stopping thumping noise and saw the huge animal coming toward him. It stopped to look around. Zack was scared to even move but lucky the animal moved away for some reason. Zack let out a sigh of relief to be safe. He thought it was the smell of the place that scared the animal away. Zack then got a big stick and walked around a bit and wanted to think but he couldn't. He was hungry and had to find food soon before night came and it was sunset.

Zack had luck on his side and found some fruit but it kind of looked like something a mutant would eat. He had to eat it in order to think of a plan to reach the future or to get back to his time. For now he would have to survive the nature that was before him. The huge animals and tiny animals would screech and scratch at him. He saw something swoop down and start to eat something. Zack thought, "Oh great, now there goes some of my food that I was going to eat!" Suddenly he was swooped off his feet and into the air. He kicked and kicked around to be released from the talons but it was no use.

Watching the ground move below him made him sick, he thought what kind of animals are these? Were they regular animals not found yet? Or were they from the sea? If they were, where was human life? Trees were the only thing he could see - huts? It looked like Indians made in their time. Zach wondered, "Unless this is the future for mankind? Weird animals and huts for us to live in but that can't be possi-" he was dropped into a nest landing among eggs. Giant eggs and he felt them. He saw them begin cracking open. He backed away and saw birds. At first they seemed confused, then mother came down for a landing. She saw Zack - and the birds looked hungry and so he didn't have to think.

Zack ran across cliffs and mountains he had never seen before and thought, "Hmmm the strange mountains with birds flying around them." The baby birds were catching on to him so he looked below him. A river! He could jump in it and the mutant babies wouldn't be able to fly yet. But the problem was, he didn't know if they could fly. He was terrified that he would be swooped up by the mother. He jumped. The babies started crying for food and the mother was angry – she was coming in fast, but Zack finally hit the water and the beast flew away.

Zack had little hope for that plan to work but it did. When he landed he was astonished to find gentle beasts eating exotic plants. They stared at Zack as if he was a threat. Zack slowly moved among the beasts without harming them or startling them. He could easily be squashed into the ground with their hideous looking feet. So Zack carefully continued his journey to find shelter and food. He moved so quietly and carefully that the animals didn't even think to hurt him while he looked for food.

By Joe Brown

Bike.
Crank, rims,
Tires, frames, bars,
Pegs, headset, forks, grips,
Hub guard, chain guard,
Hubs, sprocket,
Chain.

Bike frames
Stolen,
Eastern, Fit,
Dk, Sobrosa, Verde,
2-Hip, We The People, Black Eye,
Colony, Deluxe, Haro,
Mirraco, Federal,
Fly.
Get one!!

I Miss You

By: Sarah Ciminillo

I really miss you,
Every time I think about you I get sad,
If only I was with you,
I would be glad!
All the memories
Like fishing off the boat,
Or that one time you fell in the water,
And tried to float!
You watching me on the trampoline,
Doing exotic tricks, just jumping away,
You were so amazed,
You didn't know what to say!
Building the tree house,
You, Becca, and I
When I think about the memories,
I let out a sigh
When baby Lewis came along,
I remember singing him a song
Him trying to talk and letting out coos,
I was so excited,
I told you all the news!
I want things back to the way they used to be,
So our lives would be worry-free,
You leaving, just going away,
I'm hoping that you will come back, one day
Dad, I love you and you will always be in my heart,
It's too bad we are so far apart

Rosy
By Cheyenne Comerford

In April of 2008, I started volunteering at the Equine STAR Horse Rescue, in White Lake. I did a few riding camps and made a bunch of new friends. I also got so much better at riding. I would go there and clean out stalls and work with the horses almost every day, every week. In November, after I had been volunteering for about six months, seven new horses came. No other horse rescues would take them because there was a mare, two stallions, two yearling fillies (a young mare), and two pregnant mares. Joan, the founder of Equine STAR, didn't have enough room or money for horses but she still took them because she couldn't stand to see them go to auction or be put down. I am really happy that she did take them because one of them would become my best friend.

The first time I saw them, I fell in love with one of the fillies. She was a year and a half old and her name is Rosy. She is a bay tobiano American Paint Horse. I started working with her right away. About a week later, Joan took me to Milford Laundry so I could help wash horse blankets. We were talking and she told me that I should adopt Rosy because she worked so well for me and I absolutely loved her! It took me about a week to convince my parents to let me adopt her. They both loved her too so it was pretty easy. I worked with her almost every day and she was doing so well and improving every time. I had to train her to stand still so that I could groom her, pick up all four feet and be able to put a blanket on her. I also had to teach her some manners and how to lounge. She had been halter and lead broke by her former owners so I didn't have to teach her those. There were so many other things that I had to train or teach her to do. It was a lot of work but it was worth it!

If I was going to show her that coming show season, I had about five months to get her ready. I had to teach her all of the showmanship maneuvers and get her really good at them. I also had to get her in shape for the halter classes. In a halter class, the horse is judged on their conformation or how they are built. In showmanship, the class is judged on the person and how well they can control their horse's moves and how much training the horse has, all from on the ground. We ended up doing really good for our first year of showing. The best we got was a 3rd place out of 14 horses in a halter class. I was so excited!

I have had Rosy for over a year and a half now. She has taught me just as much as I have taught her. We moved her to a really nice barn in September of 2009 because the horse rescue was in foreclosure and closing in a couple of months. We both love it there! I am going to continue showing her and I will start riding her in May 2010, when she turns 3. She is better than a lot of the older horses at the barn and has been improving in all of her training every time I work with her. For me, she is the best horse ever!

Broken Arm
By: Bradley Conklin

In the year 2005 I was playing tag outside on recess.
I was in the third grade, at Houghton elementary school.
I was running, I got to the stairs on the play structure and jumped. I had a sharp pain in my right arm, it felt as though someone stabbed my arm with a red hot blade. I looked down in fear to find my right arm bent down.
I had to go into surgery, and have a cast for two months, but at least my arm healed up.

Broken Arm

Arm.

    Broke, bent.

        Running, jumping, falling.

            It was tag on recess.

                Useless Appendage.

Broken Arm

Broke.

    Jump, fall.

        Crying, running, screaming.

            Houghton Elementary school,

                White Lake Michigan,

        cast, medicine.

            Healed, repaired.

GREAT NFL DUOS
By Logan Cook

When you hear duo you think of two people but when you hear NFL duos you think of Jerry Rice and Joe Montana or Peyton manning and Reggie Wayne. All duos are good in one way or another, but not even close to being as good as the duos. The NFL is very hard to succeed in with two people let alone yourself. These duos made the unimaginable imaginable by shattering the records one by one.

One of the greatest duos in NFL history was Joe Montana and Jerry Rice. They played for the 49ers and won 4 super bowls together. They made two miraculous comebacks together. They were unstoppable, because both of them were models of work ethic, intensity, and execution; they combined to become the foundation of the 49ers four Super Bowl teams. Joe and Jerry are considered to be the greatest and most dangerous passing game in NFL history.

The Colts Peyton Manning and Reggie Wayne are the ultimate duo because they broke all the passing records and virtually bought their way into the record books. They passed passing records, touchdown records and every other record imaginable by working together and getting the job done.

Great NFL duos that I have mentioned are great players who make the game how we know it today. Each player in the NFL is inspired by the duos of the NFL. Everyone will know who Joe Montana and Jerry Rice were and who Peyton Manning and Reggie Wayne are for generations of football fans to come.

A Baseball Story
By: Jacob Coudret

Me, personally - I play shortstop which usually gets the most balls hit to it. It's usually the hardest position to play. But this time I wanted to tell the story of one of baseball from a first baseman's point of view and a catchers' point of view because everyone thinks that the catcher and first baseman have the easiest job on the baseball field. This is to prove you people wrong.

Coach is calling out what positions to play out in the field. "Jason go to first!" Coach shouted.

"Why do I always have to play first? All I do is stand there or cover the bag, the ball is never hit to me." I thought to myself. A ball is hit to shortstop, I cover the bag and it's thrown to me, I hear the ump scream "out."

Finally after five innings a lefty pinch hits for the pitcher. There is a guy on first so we have a chance for a double play. The ball is hit to me. I have to dive to even have a chance at making the play. I throw the ball to second to have a chance at a double play. The umpire screams "out." It's thrown on to first for the double play.

Bottom of the seventh, runners are on first and third two outs. The runners take off. I can hear coach yelling, "Bunt, bunt, bunt!" I sprint down the first base line, "faster, faster" is what I'm thinking. I pick the ball up barehanded, the only play I had was at home plate. I threw it home, the kid slid. After the dust cleared the ump screamed, "out!" We won that day 5-3. After that play I wanted to play first every game.

So how about other positions?......

"Justin, go catch for Matt!" coach shouted.

"Yes! I love playing catcher!" I thought to myself. The first pitch of the game was a fastball on the outside corner. I could hear the umpire scream, "Strike one!" The second pitch was a circle change hit on the ground to Jacob at shortstop. He threw it to first, the umpire screamed, "Out!" The second batter stepped up to the plate, Matt struck him out with three straight fastballs. The next hitter stepped up to the plate and he was a power hitter, but unexpectedly he laid down a bunt I picked it up and threw it to first for the third out.

I'm hitting third this inning. The first two hitters are on first and second, I hit the ball to left field for a two run double. The next three batters flew out. But I tagged up and scored from third on the second fly out.

The next inning there was a guy on first with no one out. The hitter hit a ground ball to Jacob at shortstop, he flipped it to Grady and he threw to first but the runner was safe. So it was the same situation but there was one out. The next hitter trotted up to the plate he had a hit every appearance he had at the plate and he had scored all the team's runs. Matt pitched the ball, the batter hit a ground to second he flipped it to Jacob and he through on to first.

It's the top of the seventh inning we're up to bat and the score is 3-3, the batting lineup this inning is Jacob, Grady, Brendan, then me. Jacob had hit a double, Grady singled and Jacob scored, Brendan singled, I doubled, and Grady scored. The next three batters flew out.

It's the bottom of the seventh and our team is winning 5-3. The next batter stepped up to the plate and he was a power hitter and he had a homerun already this game. Our closer Justin was on the mound. The first pitch was hit to deep center field, to the warning track to the wall, and it is caught Brendan robbed him of his second homerun on the day. The next hitter grounded out to first. The next hitter on the first pitch lined it into left center, we thought he was going to stop at third with Brendan's arm, But he kept going B threw it to Jacob for the cutoff. He gunned it to me and the ump screamed "out!" Sting win.

Buzzer Beaters
By: Phillip Cross

Kobe Bryant dribbles down the court with seconds left; he pulls up with his hands cocked and lets it fly for the win at the buzzer...swoosh! He did it! He wins the game for the Los Angeles Lakers. What a performance and game from the great one.

Buzzer Beaters. One of the most awesome and crazy shots ever done in the game of basketball. They can make peoples' jaw-drop and can change the style and pace of the entire game. In all levels from High school, college, and even the NBA, buzzer beaters just cannot be topped! I have had a few of those in my days of playing basketball. I'll tell you, there's no better feeling of hitting a game winner in front of lots of people, that's for sure!

I bet that if you ask any pro player that has hit a buzzer beater; they will tell you that it's one of the most memorable things in their career. Those kinds of feelings and emotion never leave us. The sights, sounds, and intensity of the game can not be matched by any other game.

Sports announcers on TV really make these moments more intriguing. When shots go up and are nailed at the buzzer, they go "Wow!" or "That's a phenomenal shot!" It really makes people's heads turn. These announcers make the shot even more exciting and amazing than it is. It just wouldn't be the same without an earth shattering, "Oh my god!"

Basketball is one sport that you just can't get enough of. It has all of the things you would need to meet your desire. Just seeing the big red light surrounding the backboard go off, the ball slowly going up into the air, and wondering where it might drop is just one huge thinker. Your heart pounding, eyes getting big, everyone quiet. It's all a matter of time before the crowd goes insane!

Friendship
By: Devvon Crowder

Friendship is important because you can see who your friend is in a way that other people can't. They tell you things that no one else may know. Your friend has a bond with you that others don't and usually can't have. People can be totally different and still be best friends because they know that person for who that person really is. My friend hates skateboarding, but because I like it he still does it. And then most of the time I go biking with him.

Friends can, sadly, grow apart really quickly. Most have that one or two activities that they do a lot with each other. If one doesn't like that activity anymore there friendship can start to fade away. But when they do that activity, there friendship blossoms with the joy of your friend being with you. Although you might move away, go to a new school, or just not be allowed to see them anymore you want them to be your friend no matter what the problem is. Like me being grounded and not being able to see my friends anymore sucked, but when I went to school I was able to see them as much as I wanted to.

Although friends come and go through our lives, we still need them. Friends are important because they are there for us and then most of the time we are there for them. Sadly, they come and go but there will always be that memory of a certain friend we will cherish for a long time. Try to treat your friends how you would like to be treated be cause that can make a really strong relationship. When I treat my friend how I like to be treated, me and her end up spending more time together out side of school.

Best friends?
By: Jordan Dalton

I thought

you thought

We are best friends…..

We always will be!

Middle school, new classes…..

New friends.

I don't like your new friends…..

I don't like yours either!

Let's work it out, talk?…..

Gotta go to my boyfriend's house!

Boyfriend?…..

Yes!

Wait, what? Boys have cooties!…..

No they don't!

Yes, don't you remember they
Would try to play with us on recess
And we would run?…..

Well they're cool!

But what about me?…..

What about you?

What's going on?…..

Why are you being like that?

Being like what? I want to hang out with you….. **I'm busy right now.**

Why are you letting him take you away?…..

**You're just jealous of
my new life**.

No, I just want you back!…..

If you don't like it you can go.

No, I'm not going anywhere!…..

**Well my boyfriend doesn't
want me around You anymore.**

What?….

**you heard me, I don't want to hang out with
You anymore, Make it easy and just leave.**

I can't just leave like that. I wont!….. **Okay, well bye.**

No! You're just going to leave me like that?….. **Yeah.**

Ahh, I hate him….. **Well I don't, I love him!**

You don't even know what that means….. **Yeah I do.**

I won't let you push me away. I will be here waiting….. **There's nothing to wait for.**

Yes there is….. **What then.**

You…..
    I will always be here for you no matter what! Even if your not here for me!…..

Fourth Grade's Pains
By: Marji Dean

Every bump, every jolt sent pain searing through my knee. Why my teacher had to send me home on the bus instead of calling my mom, I have no idea. It would have been way easier. Instead, here I am, sitting on the bus, crying, in pain, willing to give anything to get off this bus, and knowing for a fact that I am going to need stitches, but there is a giant band-aid on my knee, making it almost impossible to walk. While I sit here, I definitely have some time to think. Looking back, I wish that I had never gone onto that track....

Fall 2006. It was warm and sunny. When I woke up on this glorious morning, I decided to wear my favorite outfit: a white shirt with ruffles, a purple plaid skirt, and my new pair of "cowboy boots", at least, that's what I called them. I didn't bother putting on tights; it was going to be warm today, my dad had said, and anyways, I didn't have a pair that would work, one was too thick for anytime but the middle of January, the other one would not match, seeing as it was green as grass. I went to school as happy as could be, anticipating a fun-filled day, not knowing that I would soon not be enjoying the weather or talking to my friends.

Every day in fourth grade was joyous, because my most favorite teacher in the world was teaching me: Mrs. Sheiman. We always started the day with Language Arts, which I have loved since the age of four. We would then do a little bit of Math, and then it was time for recess. Then we would be called in by the playground monitors and eat lunch, then, if we had time afterwards, we would be allowed to go outside for a little while longer. We'd do our other subjects after lunch, and after we would go back outside for second recess. On this particular day, our class had earned extra recess time, probably because of our good behavior.

During recess I had decided to play with my friend Liz in "the field", a field of grass between two baseball diamonds. Since we were little kids, all we were doing was running around, flapping our arms and screaming nonsense words into the air. (But that's common among fourth graders, right? Really? Its not? Well then, just goes to show you what I was like when I was a little kid....)After a while of being idiots I tired of the game, so I decided to go and play with some of my other friends. If I only knew where they were... I felt like starting at the blacktop, so I started running in the direction of a track smack dab in the middle of the playground, cut across one part of it to the far side of the track, and jogged down it. I passed the blacktop where some of my friends were either skipping rope or playing four-square. Bo-ring! I was never very fond of those games, so I kept jogging past them, and kept on going until I reached the swings, where some of my friends were laughing and screaming and jumping of at the highest point that they could go, seeing who could go the farthest. I did like going on the swings, but my parents had told me to never swing while wearing a skirt, and anyways, there were no open swings, so I kept on jogging past them. Then I spotted the Big Toy. Perfect. Everyone played over there all the time, so at least a few of my friends were bound to be over there that were willing to play with me. I set off.

Suddenly, I felt myself flying forward; the pavement was flying towards me. Instinctively, I threw out my hands.

BAM!!!!!!!

My knee was hurt. Badly. I knew I was scraped up a bit, but not how much. I felt myself skidding forward a couple inches. And then I felt the pain. Agonizing pain. Excruciating pain, in my right knee. And my hands. But not as much. I heard people screaming, but for all I knew the screaming was from all the other kids playing, or flying off their swings. I sat up and looked around.

Mrs. Sheiman was running towards me, looking worried. As well as a couple other people.

Thankfully Mrs. Sheiman came to my rescue quickly, before a crowd could form, asking if I was all right, if I could stand up. I told her that my knee hurt, and started crying hard. She helped me to my feet, and made a hissing noise, looking at my knee. I looked down, and cried even harder.

The skin of my knee had disappeared, tucked under some other skin. There was a lot of blood, you could see my muscle, and in some places, bone.

I looked down at the track, thinking that there would be a blood stain there, but instead, a little bit back, where I had tripped, I saw a crack in the asphalt. I probably had tripped on it when I was skipping. Then my vision blurred so bad that I couldn't see anything.

Mrs. Sheiman put her arm around my shoulders and helped me walk to her classroom. Mercifully, her back door was open, or else we would have had to go through the main door and walked through the hall, and then everyone would have seen how badly hurt I was. She sat me down on the counter next to the sink and the drinking fountain, and told someone to call everybody in from extra recess. After a while my crying slowed down a bit, and I was able to see Mrs. Sheiman rummaging through her desk drawer for something. She straightened up after a bit, and came over to me with a giant knee bandage. At this time everyone was coming in to the classroom, heard someone crying, turned around, and when they saw me there, they started talking to each other. My friends all came to me and asked me what happened and if I was okay, but all I could do was nod and cry. My friend Liz came into the room and came over to me. Now I wish that I had stayed with her and played the Idiot Game or something, but Fate had led me to pain, and I felt then that Fate was definitely not my friend, because he had hurt me.

Mrs. Sheiman put the band-aid on my knee, and asked me if I could walk with it on. She helped me stand up, and I wobbled slightly on one foot, and then I gently set my foot down.

"OWWWW!!!!!!"

Yeah. I definitely can walk on this. Mm-hmm. Yep. Not really, no.

Mrs. Sheiman came over to me and told me to walk a space forward. I tried, but I could only hop. I tried a couple times, and finally I could set my foot down gingerly. After a couple more tries I could walk on it a little distance. After that, I couldn't go any farther. There was too much pain.

Suddenly, I heard the bell ring. It was time to go home! I didn't even have my stuff out of my locker!

Mrs. Sheiman helped me to my locker and got my stuff out of my locker for me, gave me my coat, and saw me out the door.

Half hopping, half limping, I went to the bus, my face still streaked with tears. I thankfully made it to the white bus line before they headed out. I was still at the back of the line, but I had made it in good time.

I couldn't rest long, though. The line suddenly started moving forward, and the person in front was marching forward proudly, holding the white laminated circle on a yard stick in the air. I started hopping forward, fresh tears pouring silently down my face. I wobbled and almost fell on my face. Well, I can't hop anymore. Better stick to walking, no matter how painful it will be, because it will hurt to walk. I took a step forward, and there wasn't as much pain as last time when I tried to walk. I took another step, gingerly. I felt more pain. Better start limping.

I made it to the bus, going at a steady pace, and used the handrail to hop up the stairs. I found an empty seat, but then someone else came onto the bus and I had to share it. I sat down in the aisle way while the other person sat by the window. After about a minute, the bus started forward.

There were two other bus stops before mine. Every one of them was longer than the first, and all were agony.

Finally, we came to my stop. I wish that the stop was in front of my house like it was last year, but now it was at the end of the street. I waited for everyone to get off, then stepped into the aisle and limped off the bus. My sister was waiting for me, and when she saw my tear-streaked face she launched into talk, asking me bazillions of questions, like little second graders do. I just ignored her and concentrated on walking.

When we got to my house, I noticed that my mom was home from work. I let my sister walk ahead of me, and then I went in. I dropped my stuff on the kitchen table, and instead of calling out hello as I usually did, I just sat down in a chair.

Naturally, little Gracie the tattletale had already ran to my mom and told her that I was hurt. She came out in the kitchen and saw me sitting there crying in a chair. Her eyes gravitated to my knee, and she immediately went into mommy mode, had me sit onto the table, and called my dad from downstairs. He came up and saw me sitting on the table, with a giant band aid on my knee, and came over and took it off.

When my parents saw my knee, they cried out in alarm and launched into a bazillion questions like my sister had done. I told them the whole story, and my mom got a clean knee bandage, and took all of us to the emergency center, which I knew well.

When we got to the center, my mom pulled up to the doors, and my dad got out and got me a wheelchair from inside. He opened my door and set me gently into it, and rolled me into the building.

Inside, everything was bright and clean-looking. My mom signed us in and came back, and after a while we were called. My dad decided to stay in the waiting room, and we went ahead. We were sent into a waiting room and the doctor came in after a bit. He took one look at me, with my bandaged knee, and took it off. He saw my knee, and sent us to the surgery room. He set us up in a room with a bed and curtain, and my mom laid me on the bed. The doctor took some iodine and numbed up my knee. He waited a while and then took out this wicked looking needle, all curved and gleaming. My mom saw me looking faint, and gave me a magazine to look at. I soon felt a tugging at my knee, and looked over, and saw the needle in my skin. I quickly looked away and waited until the doctor was done. Then he cleaned my knee and said that I could go home now. We went into the waiting room and got my dad and went home.

The next day I was really popular. Everyone wanted to see my knee. I became the center of attention. I repeated my story so many times it was beat into my brain and I finally got tired of reliving the story, so I refused to tell it anymore.

Now all I have of that scary day is memories. That, and a scar on my knee.

Miss You Two.
By: Chloe Denton

I wish I was able to tell you how I felt.
Every second of every day I'm missing you both.
I don't know what it is about you, but you just keep me.
I know everything *seems* so great when we're talking,
when we are just sitting in silence or when were not even together.
But honestly, I'm getting torn apart on the inside,
and noone but me sees that pain.
Sometimes I let it get too me,
sometimes you ask me, "What's wrong?"
But it's not *all the time* that you ask me what's wrong,
even though there is something wrong, all the time.
I want you to know everything,
and I want you to care again.
Remember when nothing at all could come between us?
When *they* didn't care if we talked in the halls or outside of school?
They didn't want your friendship as badly as I needed it.
We would hangout on the weekends
and you didn't have any other plans with other little groups,
because there were none.
Cliques have torn all of us apart,
and noone else seems to notice it,
maybe I care too much,
or maybe you don't care enough.
I still wish we were best friends like before,
I still don't have anyone that's there for me like you two were.
I won't ever be able to replace you two.

My Hobbies
by: Jimmy Derocher

Biking,
Dirt, street,
Stairs, rails, trails,
Roads, burms, walls, jumps,
Fit, Stolen, Verde,
Fly, Eastern,
Biking

Soccer,
Cleats, shin guards,
Jerseys, refs, goalies,
Goals, shots, save's, passes,
Throw- ins, pk's, corners,
Punts, headers,
Soccer

Baseball the Best Sport in the World!
By Avery Dudek

Game
catching, tossing, running
Tigers, Red Socks, New York Yanks
exciting, exercising, entertaining
intense, adrenaline pumping
America's favorite pastime

Baseball
flying, soaring, bouncing
leather, seams, stitching, smooth
toss, throw, catch
wind, dust, grass
Hardball

Pitching
throwing, bobbling, fielding
Verlander, Zumya, Porcello, Coke
fun, sweat breaker, athletic
thrilling, amazing, mind working
Reliever

Bat
hitting, driving, smashing
easton, worth, plasma, stealth
swung, tossed, dropped
dusty, chipped, dented
Stick

Always

By: Cameron Dunn

You and I have had our rough patches in the past,
                  times when we were apart.
I've always felt like an outcast,
                  felt deserted, neglected, and abandoned.
You've shown me strength when I couldn't be strong,
                  helped me with pressure of resentment
You've always watched me so I could never be steered wrong,
                  not to give up and to stay out of the wrong crowd.
You fought for me as though you were a soldier fighting in a war,
                  fought for the time we have together.
I know the divorce was hard but I will always be your son that's a matter a fact,
                  I love you mom.
                  You were and will always be my hero.

2012: Milo's Story
By: Kayla Elton

2012, when I think about what's predicted to happen that year, a shiver runs down my spine. Many people believe that it's just a coincidence that on December 21, 2012 there will be a winter solstice. Venus will move in front of the Sun causing a Galactic alignment, and the Mayan calendar will end. Personally, I don't believe it's just a coincidence.

July 19th 2012
My name is Milo and I am 11 years old. I live in Sacramento, California. My parents are scientists; they have been studying the Apocalypses of 2012 for as long as I can remember. They aren't allowed to talk about what they find; the government thinks the only way to keep order is not to talk. Sometimes they break that rule and tell me.

August 6th 2012
There is very little food now and the world is in a state of shock. We have more money than other people, which means more food. For others, they're getting by on as much as they can afford. Many people have died. Many countries populations are completely wiped out.

September 23rd 2012
They told me. That's when I realized why my parents were working late everyday over the summer. I was mad at first, why hadn't they told me! Mom said they had to be sure, she didn't want me to worry about anything; dad said that we knew, that we've known for hundreds of years.

September 24th 2012
I went to school today. My best friend April was waiting for me by the fence at the end of my street. As I walked, I heard the crunching of rocks and sand beneath my feet. It was hot, it always was. I visited Wisconsin when I was 5, it was cold and there was snow. I went last year and it was as hot as it was in Sacramento. I walked up to her; she just looked at me, her dark brown eyes longing to know what I knew. I wanted to tell her, but I couldn't. She had asked me what was wrong, I said nothing, but I knew she could tell, she was good at that.

October 15th 2012

I spend a lot of my time outside with April; since about three years ago they stopped giving us homework because the tree population was decreasing. Lots of days we just talk, but some days when it's not too hot, we play street hockey, which can get pretty intense! But we never talk about what's going to happen in a few short months.

November 28th 2012

My parents came home so happy. I couldn't believe they could be that happy with the 21st coming up. But when they told me that many scientists around the world, including them, had discovered a way to reverse the age of the Earth I couldn't believe it. They said that by making the Earth younger, in turn would make everything okay, not really in those words but I couldn't understand it, I just hope it works.

December 16th 2012

The scientist finished what they were doing to the Earth, the effects of it will start taking place in 23 minutes, many people will die from it, but some will live. If I make another entry, the world will know that I lived. They will know my story.

My Dog Riley

by: Jason Fairbrother

This is my dog
He likes to run
He is brown; black; and white
This is my dog
He is friendly to all
And is tons of fun.

This is my dog
He is soft
He is fuzzy
He is strong
And he is fast.

This is my dog
Sometimes he gets on my nerves
But I love him and he loves me too.

This is my dog his Name is Riley.

Dad
By James Fish

I sit here in class writing this poem
trying to figure out when everything went wrong.
Its Four years later and I still don't want to believe it.
I didn't believe it when we got that call,
one call changed everything.

It didn't strike me until I saw you lying in your casket.
Flowers were there so were friends, old pictures of good memories,
and old pictures of good friends,
but through all the comforting everyone tried to do,
none of it could bring back you.

Everyday I mourn your passing,
and I still can't get over all the stuff that happened.
So I sit here in class trying to write a poem, trying to remember you…
Dad.

School Daze Part: 1
By: Marianna Fisher

"I'm never doing that, ever!" I shouted at my teacher. She had called me up to get a detention for tomorrow, because I refused to go to the office. My name's Justin and my school is Pierce. I never really get detentions at all, not even for dumb things.

"Why did you get a detention for not going to the office?" my friend Cameron asked later at lunch.

"Well maybe you should have asked what you were supposed to get for her from the office!" Michael said.

"I'm never asking her that dumb question!" I said. We decided to not talk about it any more. It was a dumb situation anyways.

I brought home the detention slip for my parents to sign. They said to skip it altogether.

"What are you going to do about this?" Chris asked.

"I'm going to skip it!" I said proudly. That's what I did. When the teacher asked why I had skipped it.   I didn't say a word and she just gave up on it. She decided to start the lesson like she always does. But, right in the middle the principle came down. He handed her some test copies that she never gotten from him. She took them nervously and he left the room.

She started right where she was with the math lesson. At the end of class she calls me up and says sorry to me. I say sorry for not getting the test copies from the principle. After school I go to Taco Bell and ordered a burrito for myself. I get home and eat it up in 10 minutes.

The next day at school I saw I was on the all "A" honor roll! I immediately told my friends and they were happy for me. I even got compliments from all my teachers and I thanked them. I was so happy I had gotten on the honor roll. I got a cookie at lunch to celebrate this moment.

My Baby Brother
By Amanda Flowers

I don't know whether I can believe it when people tell me my baby brother will be fine. The doctors all say he has a seventy percent chance of getting better. They say no need to worry, but I just can't help thinking what if he's that other thirty percent? What if he can't fight it? What if he's not brave enough or strong enough? Then what? I just watch him fade away?

I want to believe them but I just can't convince myself to. The thing is, people say you have to be strong, right? Well, I'm not exactly sure if he is. The night before and the day of chemo, he sits and sobs his little eyes out saying how much he wants to die all because he doesn't want to go to the hospital and be in pain. For a ten year old, I think that's pretty bad. Even after he gets home he's sick all day long and when he has to go back to the hospital that's when everything gets worse. My mom's always gone, Aussie's always gone. I miss them.

I don't know how hard things are going to get, but I just don't think I'm ready for more. I just can't bare it. I want everything to be back to normal. I want to know he's brave enough to fight this. It's hard to know what's going through his mind besides being sick and depressed all the time. Just the way he walks you can tell he is in pain. You can see it in his eyes, all the hurt and misery he goes through every day. I just wish it would all blow over soon.

Pieces of a broken heart
By: Emily Flowers 4th L.A.

You are my life, my world, my "boo".
I'm only able to love you.

I can't move on, I can't go back, unless every thing I've been fighting for will have been a waste.

I'll fight for you with every fiber of my being. I will never give up, until I take my last breath, which doesn't even matter without you, every breath is a breath I take is a breath I'll take alone.

My hearts in sorrow, weeping with anger, sadness, pain, and emptiness, but all at the same time it's also alone, worried, and scared,

Scared that I'll never see you again,

Scared that I will live alone forever.

I need you back. Every second without you is an eternity. A Lifetime passing me by without the slightest little glance.

I need you, I Love you, I'm sorry, and whatever I said to make you leave, I take it all back.

Just come back to me I need you baby.

People call every little fling love but there just caught in the moment, once its gone you just move on but true love stays forever, even long after they're gone.

You make my heart beat faster and slower all at the same time. I need you to hold my hand, so that I can make it through the day, without shedding a tear, I can only do that with you.

I also need somebody to carry me through it all.

I Love you please come rescue me, my love I'm sorry to you but not only you, also to myself for letting you just walk right out of my life.

Even though you're gone I will always carry you right along with me.

Memories That Will Never Fade Away
By: Lauren Fluder

When I was in kindergarten my dad was diagnosed with ulcerative colitis. It's strange how having one person out of your life for a short time can really affect you. Ulcerative colitis is a chronic inflammation of the large intestine. It is hereditary, it runs in his family. My grandma has it and my dad had it. I am hoping that my brother and I won't get it. I am so glad my dad is not sick anymore because I wouldn't have had the opportunity to make all the memories I now have with him.

Even though I was only five I still remember him being in the hospital from mid November until mid January. He did not get to spend Christmas with me and my mom. When he first entered the hospital, the doctors did not know what was wrong with him until he explained his family medical history to them. The doctors then treated him immediately for ulcerative colitis. They did scopes, ultra sounds, and many tests on him. At one point, his whole body was poisoned. My dad was never told how his body got poisoned. He almost died from that poisoning but the doctors got him un-poisoned by doing a colonoscopy. (A colonoscopy is where they get rid of your large intestine.) The only way you can get rid of ulcerative colitis completely is to get rid of all your large intestine. Even though he didn't have his large intestine he was still able to digest food with his small intestine. After a few weeks of recovery and observation he was released from the hospital.

After being at home for a week he got sick again. Once again his intestine was acting up. During the night my mom called 9-1-1. When I woke up that morning my mom told me that my dad was sick again and he was back in the hospital. I remember feeling very sad when I heard that. That morning my mom and I drove to Beaumont to see my dad. When I went to walk into his room the nurses said I couldn't go in because I was too young! My mom did not listen to them; she thought I should be able to see my dad.

A few weeks later my dad had another surgery to see what was wrong. They found out the problem and fixed it. During that surgery they had to re-design his small intestine since they got rid of his big one. In the beginning of May my dad was released from the hospital for the final time! He had been in the hospital for about six and a half months.

Now he's doing a lot better; he still gets some infections from time to time. He also has to go to his colitis doctor every six months. He has to have scopes when he checks up with his doctor. The bad part about him being out of the hospital is that he had cataracts in his eyes so he had to have eye surgery to get rid of it. My dad also had to lose a lot of weight since he was not able to move a lot in the hospital and being on all of the medicines he was on. But now he is in shape again. Some of the memories I couldn't stand not having with him are, playing catch with him, going on vacations with him, going to baseball games, and him helping coach my softball team. I am very grateful that he is all better and I hope that he continues to stay healthy.

Right Hand Man
By Erich Gainer

Why, why, why? Really! Why is it always me? Why not Lefty over there?

I mean seriously, earlier today we were out canoeing in one of the river deltas on the Virginia coast. I was helping push the canoe into the water. When it was almost in the water I slipped and cut myself open on the bow. There was a slice through me the size of a lemon, leaking blood like a faucet. Man!

Because of me we all have to go back home. Trying to paddle back with the salty water splashing in my wound was not enjoyable at all. I'm getting very angry at my boss, "The Brain Man", telling me to keep working with all the pain. Also, the stress isn't helping the bleeding. But still I keep working no matter how much I want to stop.

Lefty is kind enough to take as much of the work as possible so it is easier for me to help paddle. Too bad he can't get rid of the water. Now that would be nice. That would be really nice.

This trauma suit could be changed. It's getting a little soggy from blood and water. Maybe at the next clearing we could stop and get it changed.

Even though the pain is making it hard to focus the nature is really beautiful. To bad it all had to end early.

It's all my fault. Now we all have to go home all because I slipped. Why was I so stupid. I should have seen it coming

All the way back to the launch the pain was menacing. The paddle is now starting to turn red in my grip. I just really want to get home and put a new, not so soggy, bandage on.

Finally, we made back to the launch. But now I'm going to have to help take the canoe out of the water. That's gong to be the hard part, getting in the salty water to lift the canoe out of the water and into the truck.

The Campsite Ghost
By: Kylee E. Gallero

"I don't think there is anything here Vic." I said. I was annoyed that we had not seen anything.

"My mom saw it over there, when she went to go get more wood for the fire." She replied.

"Fine we will wait a little longer, then we will drive home." We waited, and then Victoria saw something bright come out of the shadows.

"I......I... I... I told you!" Victoria stuttered.

"What are you talking about?" "I saw the ghost!" she yelped.

"Okay, nice try. You are not going to fool me that easily."

"I'm not joking. I know I saw some..." She stopped.

"What? WHAT?!?!" I cried.

"Behind you!" I turned. "Oh my...."

"Run!" she yelled. I didn't, I was frozen with fear. Neither of us could move.

We looked into the bright shining light. I saw a girls face in the middle of it.

"What the..." I said silently to myself.

She came closer to us. I laughed without thinking.

"What are you laughing at? It's a ghost." Victoria said with concern.

"I know it is. But I know it is." She was frightened by my reply.

"Look into her eyes you will know who she is too." Victoria looked into her eyes.

"Oh my... I can't believe it!" She burst out laughing at her confusion.

"See, now do you know who I'm talking about?" I asked.

Victoria nodded with relief. It was her old friend Paula.

"I feel dumb now." She had said sheepishly.

"Well at least now we can go home and you can tell your mom not to be frightened anymore." I replied.

" Yeah I know, but I kind of want to keep it just between us."

"You can, if you want to."

"I think I will." She said in relief once more.

"Cool, now let's get out of here. I have a mountain of homework to do."

We went to school the next day and everyone asked us what happened. We wanted to keep it private, but they kept pestering us all day long. They were so interested about our weekend that we got too annoyed and took them to the campsite. They thought we were crazy, but they saw her with their own eyes. They were speechless. They ran as fast as they could out of the woods. I looked at Victoria.

"Why are they so afraid? They are the ones who kept asking us about our trip." I was very annoyed.

Victoria wasn't, she was laughing so hard. She was crying at the looks on their faces. I started to laugh too, when I saw a girl pass out on the ground. Victoria went over to her and picked her up and put her into the car. We took everyone home.

"They were so scared!" Victoria burst out with laughter.

But it was so funny, that we couldn't help but to start laughing again.

We went to school the next day and our classmates avoided us for the entire day. Except one person, Jeff, he was the only one that would talk to us for some reason.

"Why aren't you avoiding us like the others?" I asked softly.

"I'm not afraid of seeing ghosts." He replied.

"Oh okay   Why not?"

"Because ghosts just don't scare me, they are really cool to me."

"Do you want to go back to the campsite with Victoria and I this weekend?" I asked.

"Sure." He replied excitedly.

"Cool. I got to go, see you later." I went and told Victoria what we were going to do over the weekend.

"This will be interesting." She replied with a smirk.

We went back to the campsite; we waited till dark and saw her once again.

"Cool!! Can I get closer to her?" Jeff asked us.

"Of course you can she won't hurt you." Victoria said excitedly.

He walked up to Victoria's glowing friend. We started to grin and giggle in anticipation. When he got close enough, we pushed him through the light and he disappeared with it.

There was one thing we didn't tell anyone, that Paula was an evil spirit. She was evil because of her past, which no body knows of, the only thing we knew of was that she was murdered by someone. But no body knew who murdered her though. But it was funny how she would make people disappear with one touch. All she was concerned with was revenge, because of her murder.

Green
By Elizabeth Goins

What has happened to our environment? Animals' homes are being destroyed, people are not helping the earth, and they are taking it for granted. When North America was founded it was a beautiful place with lots of forests and now it's a place with lots of streets, buildings and other man made things. It's like a monster clashing with the earth, and the monster is winning. Is it going to get worse? Or is it going to get better?

Animals are becoming extinct because of the way we are living. The oceans are being polluted by our waste and causing animals to die! Forests are being cut down and animals are being forced out of their habitats. The good thing is that people are trying to clean up beaches and starting groups to encourage people to be smarter and not to litter. People are also encouraging others to recycle so that animals can live peacefully in their habitats.

Humans have finally realized that the earth will not be around for very long if we keep hurting it, so people are going green! We are using products that are biodegradable so they don't hurt the earth. We are recycling paper, cans, and bottles, and not littering. We are also conserving energy by turning of faucets and lights when they aren't being used, and buying electric cars and cars that use solar energy. Celebrities are doing green things too that inspire their fan to help too. People really need to start going green before there's no time left.

Some people are taking the earth for granted and not helping. They are doing the opposite of going green (like littering, throwing away electronics, and driving gas guzzlers). The next generation might not know what to do with the environment and how to go green. That could happen to my generation as well so we need to keep helping the earth and keep adapting to the environment.

The question remains: Is it going to get worse or better? Are we going to ignore the earth's environment and let it go down the drain or are we going to adapted to it and help it heal. What ever happens I want it to turn good and have more hope in the future. Go Green!

Thunderstorm
Frances. Gorman

It was June 8, 2008, two days after my birthday. My family and I went to Pinelake. We were enjoying our Sunday afternoon, it was sunny and hot. My mom was talking to my sister Libby on the phone. Libby was across the lake at the golf course working. Libby told my mom that a thunderstorm was coming our way.

My sister and my aunt were going to go up to the house to get the car. My family and I started packing to leave. I looked across the lake and all of the sudden the sky turned a misty shade of gray and got darker very quickly. The wind was getting stronger and stronger, and I heard a crack of thunder! I looked up and saw the rain coming across the lake.

I didn't know what to do. I thought about running to the Port –A John because that would a safe place to be but then again I thought that it might tip over! (I definitely wouldn't be so happy if it did). So, I ran to my mom and we quickly tried to find shelter. We looked everywhere, but the only shelter we could find was three big trees. We stood up against the trees, and I started to cry. While standing there, I thought "this was going to be the end". I thought I was going to die slowly and painfully.

The rain continued pouring down, to make it worse it started hailing, and the wind was really strong as well. I was holding my moms hand, when we heard a loud crack. I looked behind me, one of the trees had spilt right in half! Now I was really panicking! I couldn't believe it. Under the cracked tree, somebody was calling for help but I couldn't tell who it was. My dad came out of nowhere and rushed over to the cracked tree and lifted the tree to get the person out of there.

The person was a guest at Pinelake, she was okay but she had a lot of scratches on her back. I was very relieved because the storm had finally stopped. I was still crying. This storm took my breath away. I looked around me; there were a lot of branches everywhere. I couldn't believe this happened. It was an unbelievable day. It was a day that I will never ever forget.

Soccer Story
By Austin Gothard

Got my new shoes from footlocker.

I'm ready for one of my favorite sports, Soccer.

All the trophies plenty of fame. Everyone I knew came to the game.

I've practiced I'm ready my teams undefeated. We beat the others so bad most think we cheated.

Who can stop us now, not this team? I mean come on they're not really as big as they seem.

They're only what a couple feet taller, that's the only reason we look so much smaller. We can take 'em I know we can. We can do just think, do it for the fans.

I move back ready to take my shot the last of the game if we win our school has eternal fame.

I take the shot the ball flies, hope for the other team winning dies.

The game is over and done and that's how my team won.

Broken Ankle
By Kelsea Grecu

Have you ever had one of those days where you were just tired and clumsy? Well, in the beginning of 8th grade I had one of those days coming home from school. I would like to say that it was the first time that I was ever clumsy, but I have done many klutzy things! I have fallen down the stairs and up! I've crashed my bike into a tree, fallen off my bike as well as my scooter. I have even flipped off a trampoline, just name a few of my glorious moments. Unfortunately, I have to say that this was one of the worst incidents I have ever had. It ended up leading to way more than I could have ever imagined.

I was getting off the bus, going home from school. I fell down the steps on the bus. I tried to catch myself, but it didn't work very well. I heard bones crack, and felt searing pain. I knew my ankle was broken instantly. When I tried to walk on it to go home I had terrible pain and my ankle was giving out. As I attempted to hobble home, I was thinking only of what I had just done to my ankle. It was no use I couldn't make it.

I called my mom to come and pick me up. Faster than I thought possible, she was there and whisked me off to the hospital. In the emergency room I was crying my eyes out. I had my foot x-rayed right away. The doctor said it was only a sprain. I knew it had to be something more than that! My ankle was swollen and bruised, and I was in terrible pain. But the doctor thought differently and sent me home with a splint, still crying.

A month later my ankle was no better and I had to return to the doctor. It was x-rayed again, and still they didn't find anything. But the doctor agreed there was definitely something wrong. So I was scheduled for a bone scan. It sounded good at first, until I found out that I had to get an injection! The bone scan was about an hour long, we got the results right after. The results showed that I had two breaks! The next day I got a neon orange cast. I had to wear it for three weeks.

After a week my cast started to fall apart. I went back to the doctor to have it repaired, instead they took it off. Now my ankle isn't healing correctly and I have a limp – and I have to get steroid shots in BOTH ankles! The steroid shots are really painful. The needles are long and the shots last for about a minute, and the doctor moves it around too. They spray numbing stuff on it first so all you can feel is a heavy pressure, just like your bones are breaking. Now the other ankle has problems too because I favor the one that I broke. I put all the weight on the "good" ankle. Next year 2011, I will have to have surgery on both ankles. The surgery consists of getting my bones broken, having fat put in between them, and then having them put back together. I am really nervous for it because something bad could always happen and I have never had surgery before.

Letter to Mr. Plautz
By Ricky Hack

Dear JP,

How are you? Dude, I just got done with a baseball game. I'm so sore I caught all nine innings! I was so tired but I keep on fighting I got dirty I was sweaty but it was definitely worth it. Anyways, you should have been there. I also went 4-4 with 2 H.R. and 2 doubles this made me feel so good it also brought my B.A. up but it was just a good day at the plate. I ended up having 5 R.B.I on the day. Also I scored 3 times. I threw out 4/5 of the base runners this is my new record it felt amazing hearing that ump say YOUR OUT!!! That's what kept me going. The final score was 12-1. Dude not to brag or anything but you should have seen my amazing catch. I had to run like a mile and then dive! It felt so good having that breeze in my face but when I dove I was surprised when I look in my mitt and there was the ball it was amazing. I got a standing obviation it felt so good having people chant my name I was almost in tear of excitement. Also remember bros for life and that's not going to change trust me. Also everybody knows how you are going to win the Stanley Cup, and how I'm going to win the pennant it will be so awesome and will feel so good also knowing that you will be there cheering me on and ill do the same for you. Also how we will win the M.V.P awards that will be the day when I can say we lived our life to the fullest. Well I got to go write back soon.

P.s. Tell me where and when your next Hockey game is.

Sincerely,

Ricky Hack

Collision with Disaster
By Emily Halls

"Hey, come on, slow-poke!"

"You know, just because you're fast doesn't mean that I always have to catch up to you! You know I can't handle that speed!" Miranda shouted with a smile to her best friend, Jane. They were riding their bikes up to the ice cream shop at the corner of their street. There was a huge hill tough, which is why Miranda was going so slowly. She wasn't good at riding uphill. Miranda's eyes grew wide with panic and her smile instantly faded as she saw the car coming up the road at monster speed – because Jane was still looking at her, laughing, and she knew Jane wouldn't see it in time to get out of the way.

"JANE! LOOK OUT! THERE'S A –" But she didn't finish.

A car slammed into Jane's bike on the side like the driver didn't even know, much less care, that there was a girl there. Jane was tossed off of her bike like a rag doll being thrown by a child. Her arms and legs flew through the air trying to resist the inevitable fall; the pull of gravity bringing her closer to injury. Her screams were silenced as she hit her head on the sidewalk with a crack. Miranda jumped off her bike.

"JANE! JANE! OH MY GOD JANE! JANE ARE YOU OKAY!?" Of course she knew the answer. Jane was obviously not ok. As the blood oozed onto the road, Miranda whipped out her cell phone and called 9-1-1.

"Operator, what is your emergency?"

"Please, you have to help us! My friend was just hit by a car! She's unconscious and she's bleeding; oh, and she hit her head on the sidewalk!" She gave the operator their location, and began to sob. "It'll be ok, I promise. I called an ambulance." Miranda assured her through her tears and shaky breaths. Even though she was unconscious, she hoped Jane could somehow hear her, and know that she wanted her to be ok. She sat down close to Jane, and looked away. She couldn't stand the sight of her best friend's blood below her. Just then, she heard the unmistakable siren.

They loaded Jane into the back of the ambulance on a stretcher, and they put her in a head brace. Miranda climbed in the front seat with the EMT.

"Sh-she'll be ok, right?" Miranda uttered weakly.

The driver didn't answer.

Miranda visited Jane every day in the hospital. She was in for about two weeks. Jane had cracked her skull and had needed stitches, but she had the needed procedures done, and had resting time. Jane told her stories about the doctors, and the hospital food, and the weird people who walked around in their hospital gowns. Miranda laughed, but it hurt Jane's head, so she tried not to.

"Oh my gosh, no way! You actually saw that?" Miranda giggled.

"Oh, totally! The guy didn't have the back of his gown tied up, and he was like, 70!" The girls giggled together. Then, one of Jane's attending doctors came in, and said visiting hours were over.

"Aw, already?" whined Miranda. She sighed. "Ok, guess I'll see you tomorrow." She said with a smile. As she stood up, Jane grabbed her wrist.

"I never really thanked you, you know. So thanks." Jane smiled gently, and it brought tears to Miranda's eyes. She leaned down to give her a hug and said,

"You're welcome."

GETTING BIT BY A DOG
By Justin Hart

I was five when I got bit by this dog. We were at a reception for one of my dad's friends, he was getting married. I did know anyone, so I was shy, and would not talk to anyone if they said "HI" to me. All the kids were playing with the dog when the owner asked if we wanted to feed the dog a hamburger. We all said yes. He gave us a piece of hamburger and when Jake was feeding the dog, the dog jumped to get the hamburger and Jake jerked the hamburger away from the dog. The dog lunged forward and bit me in the top lip! When the dog bit me, I fell onto the ground and, then immediately got back up and went looking for my mom and dad.

I was trying to find my mom and dad, and everyone was just staring at me. No one would help me find my parents. When I couldn't find them for about five minutes, I started to panic. But when I found them, they were on the other side of the house talking to some friends, when they heard someone screaming, they turned around and seen me and then seen the bite from the dog. My mom got the car, and my dad grabbed me and a couple of napkins. He threw me in the car and we were on are way to the hospital. On the way to the hospital I was crying and screaming because it hurt so bad. My dad used so many napkins that his lap was full of them. After we go to the hospital my dad toke me in and my mom went and parked the car and then meet use in the room were they were doing the stitches.

The dog tore my top lip on the outside so it was hanging down. Getting them stitches was the worst part about this. That fish hook like needle hurt's when they punch it threw your skin, I would scream at the top of my lunges, every time they would put it through my top lip. I had 42 stitches total. But in the end I know I could not blame the dog it was Jake that I had to blame. At the end I got a Popsicle, so I was happy then. The Popsicle was so cold that when I toke a bite it would give me a brain freeze. But they gave me the Popsicle because they wanted the stitches on the inside to freeze so they did come undone when I was eating something that that would make them come out. The Popsicle was one of my favorite flavors and it was gone in five minutes. The people at the hospital were so nice that if that ever happened to me again I would rather go there than anywhere else. The hospital was nice, it looked liked they just cleaned it and just got done with the cleaning. The nurses were the best I have ever had when I was in the hospital. They also had the best care for people that I have ever had in my entire life.

Without you

By: Howie Hensley

My Aunt Nancy, we called Aunt Nini, committed suicide on the date of 5-18-05. Without her, nothing is the same. If it was possible, I would climb up to heaven and bring her back in a matter of seconds. She was an amazing person; she inspired the whole family and made everyone happy no matter what was wrong. She would always put herself first before anyone; she was the most unselfish person I know. She always knew how to have fun, and put smiles on everyone's face. No matter what you were doing with her was great, even if you were sitting there doing absolutely nothing with her.

Although I didn't know her for that long, every memory I can think of with her is great. When I would be around her, every moment was anything but boring. My Aunt Nini was an interesting person and was a gardener; she loved to work with flowers and gardens. She loved sunflowers, and that's how everyone memorizes her; by having sometime type of sunflower object.

I remember the last day I ever spent with my aunt, and if I would of known something like this was coming, I would of gave her the greatest time of her life, one she would remember forever. My aunt Nancy was a funny person; she knew good jokes and entertaining stories. My aunt was a great person, and is deeply missed.

Gone but Never Forgotten.
By Katherine Hewitt

On April 8th when I came home from my grandpa's house I got some bad news. My guinea pig that I have had for a long time was really sick and he might not make it. I was devastated! I went over to his cage to pet him and let him know I was there. The next few nights were hard. I stayed up with him so I could make sure he was getting water and food. It was April 12th and by then he would not eat. I started to get scared. I didn't want him to die; he was the only thing I had to talk to. So my mom took him to vet to see if they could do anything for him. They said the only thing we could do was to keep giving him water and plenty of vitamin C. For the next two days I kept a close eye on him. I kept giving him water and the vitamin C tablets from the vet. (I put them in his water.) On April14th he started to eat a little bit, but not much. I was happy when I saw him take a bite of an apple.

My mom said that she would watch him so I could get some sleep. I woke up the next day and my mom said that he was doing a little bit better. I was really happy to hear that. I spent the rest of the day watching over him. I fell asleep on the couch that night. I woke up and did the same thing. When I went to bed that night, it was the night of the 16th and he was eating a little more and drinking a lot, so I went to bed. I woke up the next day and he wasn't eating. I just kept giving him water. My mom had gotten home from work around 3:30. She spent sometime with him while I got ready for the day. I came out of the bathroom and she said that he's not going to make it. I looked at her like she was crazy. Tears started to run down my face, I asked my mom if I could take his cage into my room so I could be with him if he died. She said yes, and helped me take his cage to my room.

I sat with him all day, and before I knew it, it was dinner time. I went out and made my plate and took it to my room. My mom came in and asked me how he was doing. He was doing about the same as that morning. She was getting ready to run up to the store when he stared to jump around. I screamed! My mom came running into my room. She told me to hold him and not to let go. I asked why? She didn't answer, she just looked at me with a sad face. Right then I knew what was happening, he was dying. I held on to him until the end. After about five minutes of jumping and flipping, he finally stopped. He took his last breath and then there was nothing.

I screamed his name as my mom was taking him from me. She told me to go get my step dad. He went out to the backyard to find a good spot to put him. My mom and I found a box to put him in. By the time we found a box my step dad was done with the hole. We all put on our shoes walked outside to the hole. I was crying and I could barley see to walk. I was scared; I told my mom that I was going to go back inside I couldn't watch them bury him. My parents came in and gave me a sad face and went into their room. I went out to where he was buried. I put some flowers on his grave and went inside. Everyday since then I think to myself, you're all alone in this big world, its time to grow up and move on.

True Beauty
By Aiden Hibbard

It looks like a wooden black object sitting in the room;
its knobs and switches appear as decorations,
compared to the rest of it.

The rose wood fret board is beautiful,
dark brown with small colorful stones in the middle,
the light hits them with an explosion of color filling your eyes.

The shiny, gloss of the body is mesmerizing,
shiny nickel strings cross over the silver fret bars,
they gleam with intense brightness.

This is no ordinary object,
not something you would see every day,
it's one that emits the most soft and mellow tone.

Sound that surrounds me in relaxation,
sounds that must be heaven,
it cannot be duplicated.

An object that must truly be the only one of it's kind,
a guitar.

Technology Abuse
By Jack Hillman

Technology is abused. People don't realize what it's like. People think we have it so easy. Well, it's not so easy, we have a lot of trouble, and you people over use us so much. We need a break! We're not asking for much, just a little break. We're so over worked, it's so stressful, and we get used from first thing in the morning to the middle of the night. Plus, we don't even get paid for it!

UGH! This dumb hippie kid is texting first thing in the morning! It's 6:30 a.m.! Last night he was texting until 3:00 a.m. The only time I get a break is on the weekends; he stays up until 3:00 again, but sleeps until 2:30, unless someone wakes him up. At least he'll be at school soon, but does he give me a break for a full 7 hours? No! He still texts occasionally. He made me hate being a phone. I remember in the summer, he stayed up until 5:00 a.m. on the phone almost every night. I mean who does that? I feel bad for the phone the person he was talking to was using! I'm sure that phone gets it. Since he got me, things have all gone down hill. He broke all the buttons on my front, the only button that still works is the end button, now whenever he wants to call someone, he has to flip open the front. But I'm not the only one who has it rough, so does the I-Pod. He's got a hard time too, just as bad as me, maybe a little worse sometimes.

It sucks to be this kid's I-Pod, he filled me with all kinds of hippie, "oh look at me I'm so deep because I sing about love and things that are wrong with the world" music. It's disgusting; I used to be ok with his music, but he played it too much, it's like when a new song comes out that's really good, and they over play it on the radio, so you start to hate it. Where's the music I like, where's the music I want to listen to. I don't even know what he wants to listen to half the time. He'll be listening to Bob Marley or The Beatles (I told you he was a hippie) and then all of the sudden he's listening to Escape the Fate or Eminem. God it's so annoying. When he's in his room texting or on the phone, he plays me on his speakers; he plays me just as much as he uses the phone. At least I don't have that crap his step brothers' I-Pod has on it, I mean a little screaming in a song never hurt anyone, that's fine, but I mean this kids I-pod sounds like a dying giraffe, and the guitar sounds like the guy playing it is having a seizure. You can't understand a word their saying.

So now you understand the trouble of being a phone or an I-pod. It's not as easy as you think. We can't do anything to get revenge except the occasional butt dial. But people came up with key lock just to stop that. All we're saying is to give us a break sometimes.

Or get rid of key lock, because that butt dial thing used to be really fun! But you ruined it for us.

The Tears Spoke For Me
By Emily Hodge

If I could see you now there would be so many questions I would ask.
Why did you have to leave me?
Do you miss me as much as I miss you?
Did you have to go this way?
Am I going to let the tears speak for me?

I remember the moment I found out that you had passed away.
It seemed like time had frozen,
I couldn't breathe,
I didn't know what to do,
The tears spoke for me.

At the funeral we all tried to act like we were fine.
I met relatives I didn't know,
I found it funny, they looked just like me!
When it came to speaking,
Our tears spoke for us.

The reason you left is the worst of all.
I never thought it would be something you would do.
I know you're gone now and there's nothing I can do.
There's not a day that goes by that I don't think of you.
My tears speak for me.
Even though I didn't see you as much as I wish I could have, I still cared.
I miss you and love you dad.

The Close Game
By: Dylan Holland

The one game that no one thought would be close. It was the closest in NOBF history. It was the beginning of the game. The first pitch was a ball outside that was close to the strike zone. The next two pitches were a fastball down the middle but they were fouled off. The next pitch was hit, a slow roller to the third baseman the third baseman barehanded it to me at first for the out. The next batter came up and got hit by a pitch.

There is a runner on first and one out. The next batter came up to bat. The batter bunted the ball to the third baseman and he gets him out. The runner got advanced to second so now there was a runner on second with two outs. He was a power hitter and he swung on the first pitch. It was a fastball and hit it to Matt in right field, but it bounced before it got to matt. It bounced off his glove and threw a one hopper to second without his cut off. The hit scored a run so it was one to nothing. and one out with a runner on second. The next batter bunted and advanced the runner but he got out at first. There was a runner on third and two outs. The next batter came up and we struck him out in five pitches. Nothing happened after that except we scored two in the fifth inning to tie the ball game. Then the last inning came.

"Scott, go catch for Tyler." Coach said sternly. My dad is the coach. "Why do I always have to catch" I said to my self sadly. The first pitch came down and it was a fastball. "Striiiiiike one."Yelled the ump behind the plate. There was one out and then there was one strike.

Then Tyler our pitcher threw the next pitch and it was a changeup in the dirt for ball one. The count was 1and1 the pitch that he threw next was another change up and then the batter swung and missed "striiiiiiike two" shouted the ump. The batter rips the ball to left for a base hit. The next batter hit the first pitch and it went right to Dylan at second and Cody at short for a double play to end the game. It was the first game we won and every one threw there stuff in the air and the fans started clapping and yelling.

The first out was on a drop third strike on the first batter of the inning. After the game the team and I went out and had ice cream. It was our first game of the summer league. The next day we had practice and we scrimmaged a team that we lost to in our first scrimmage. Part of my team knew some of the people on the opposing team. We play on the NOBF which stands for North Oakland Baseball Federation.

My name is Chris!
By: Mercedese Jack

My name is Chris, I am three.
My eyes are swollen, I cannot see.
I must be stupid, I must be bad.
What else could have made my daddy so mad?

I wish I were better, I wish I weren't ugly.
Then maybe my mommy would still want to hug me.
I can't do wrong I cannot speak.
Or else I'll be locked up all week.

When I'm awake, I'm all alone.
The house is dark, my folks aren't home.
When mommy does come home, I'll try to be nice.
So maybe I'll only get one whipping tonight.

I just heard a car.
My dad's back from Charlie's bar.
I hear him curse, my name is called.
I press myself against the wall.

I try to hide from his evil eyes.
I'm so afraid, I start to cry.
He finds me weeping and calls me horrible words.
He says it's my fault he suffers at work.
He slaps, hits and yells at me more.
I'm almost free, heading for the door.
He's already locked it, and I start to bawl.
He takes me and throws me against the wall.

I fall to the floor, with my bones nearly broken.
His eyes are blood shot; I can tell he's been smoking.
I'm sorry I scream, but it's now much too late.
His face has been twisted into an unimaginable shape.

The hurt and the pain again and again.
Oh please, oh please just let it end.
He finally stops and heads for the door.
I lay there motionless, bawling on the floor.

My name is Chris, I am three.
Tonight my daddy abused me.

For Pete's Sake
By Lukas Jacob

Gone, left behind
To another place,
For Pete's sake,
awaiting the gates.

Memories told,
Tears mismating,
For Pete's sake,
Sadness creating.

He's happier this way,
There's no strain,
For Pete's sake,
He has no pain.

The cancer is gone,
Our life is tougher,
For Pete's sake,
He will not suffer.

HUNTING
BY:NICK KASTLER

I'M in a tree the size of a house.
I'm in camo not a blouse.
I see a deer too far to shoot.
Next to me an owl gives a hoot.

I put my arrow on the guide.
Then the arrow is ready to glide.
I hear a crunch through the trees.
Here comes a big ten point I see.

I pick up my bow and aim at the buck.
I look at his horns as I am dumbstruck.
Surely if I shoot him it will be a treat.
For me and my family to eat.

This buck I am going to take
I put the sight on him as I quake.
This buck will not be fake but real.
When I get back it will be a big deal.

Finally I let the arrow shoot off the bow
I jerk bit as the arrow flies towards a doe.
I scream in my head OH NOOOOO!!!!!!!

By TJ Katapodis

Before each summer, I try and figure out what kind of stuff I'm going to do with all my free time. It helps me so that I spend the least amount of time hanging around my house. If I spend time around my house then I get stuck with the job of baby sitting my little brother, and I really hate baby sitting him. So in order to avoid that, I need to have stuff to do all the time.

The thing I plan to spend most of my time doing is fishing which I love a lot already, but this summer is going to be even better. My Grandpa Tony's friend, Andy, is taking us on a free fishing trip down the Pere Marquette River on his giant boat, which is so big he needs a special license to haul it! We'll be catching one of three types of fish.It'sWalleye, salmon, or Trout, but I can never remember which one (even though I've been told like 50 times). My mom says that if she can find one, she's going to send me to a camp where you all you do all day is fish, which I think is an awesome idea.

My mom also told me I have to get a job this summer, but that's ok because my Grandpa Woody said set me up with one. He's starting up an animal control company, because he's retired and doesn't have anything better to do. Another cool thing about the company is that he's going to hire my uncle Phil and my cousin Kody. It's going to be a humane business too, because we'll be letting all the animals go across the street from my dads, Right into a marshy wetland.

In the woods across the road from my dad's house is a swamp that causes a big problem in the summer, mosquitoes, but were planning to do something about it this summer. Every spring it fills up with water and each summer it dries, but were going to fix the drainage pipe that go's under the road, and then hopefully the water will drain out and take the bugs with it. With them gone we can go have bon fires without getting eaten alive.

Even though there's not a swamp at my moms, the mosquitoes still manage to bite us, which makes it a lot less fun to ride my bike and hang out with my friends, but I still do. Now that I'm going to have a job, I'm going to want to ride my bike even more. That way I can go to stores and spend my money on stuff I don't really need and not feel guilty because it's my mom or dads money. Even though most of this summer I'm going to be working it isn't going to feel like it because it's all doing stuff I love in the in the open air!

Amazing Vacation
By Justina Kos

Our whole family went on a tour to Cozumel in Mexico. In Mexico there was a store by the side of the road. We saw a lot of cool houses and the stores were small and the stuff was a lot of money. We took some pictures by the colorful ocean and it was really hot outside. We also took a group picture and we bought some bottled water to keep us cool that day.

The best part of the trip was when we went swimming in the ocean with the dolphins and stingrays. The stingrays are really slimy and they feel like mushrooms. They have a stinger that is really dangerous and the stingray was really close to me and I was freaking out. The stinger was really close to me. The stinger almost touched me and I almost cried; and I bumped into the kid and we both were looking at the same one and I told him that I'm sorry that I bumped into you. Finally, I told my dad that I was going back to the boat and my dad and my sister wouldn't let me. Instead , I was trying to stay close to my dad and my sister. I held the stingray on top of my chest and the guy took a picture of me my dad and my sister. Then my mom took some pictures of me, my dad and my sister. I had an amazing time. The ocean was a funky color blue, sort of neon in color. There were a lot of dolphins in the ocean. The fish were really colorful and the ocean had salt water which is one of the reasons the fish are so beautiful.

The forest was sprawling and the flowers were different colors they were green, orange and yellow. I saw small and large lizards and they would change to different colors. I even saw butterflies flying to a tree and they went to the forest. It was a hot day when we went on the zip line. We had to wear sunscreen on our skin because there was little shade. Finally, the monkeys were little and they looked soft and they were cute.

On one stop in Honduras…..
- I went in the deep end of the roped off area of the ocean to swim with the dolphins and the dolphin was underneath me in the water.
- The dolphin touched me with his nose below the water, near my feet.
- The instructor helped me to "surf" on top the dolphin. It was a ton of fun, I wasn't even scared.

- It was by the ocean and their where fish by the deck and the dock was by the shore and their where a lot of dock s and after we where done swimming with dolphins we went to swim with another animal and it was really slimy and then we did a group photo then we watched our movie and it was really cool and my mom and my neighbor watched the video together.

- Other people should try it too because it is an awesome trip to go to and you got to give a dolphin a kiss on the nose.

- Then the dolphin was singing.

- The instructor asked us to swim in a circle with the dolphin.

- The instructor told us to line up in a circle in the water. The dolphin started to sing, dance and also waved goodbye to us.

- On the cruise we had 12 in our cruise and we did lot stuff like the zip line and going on tours like going to the beach.

Emily M. Gilbert

By: Lauren Kozlowski

Someone to keep you busy,
When you have nothing to do.
Someone you can ask anything,
When you haven't got a clue,
Someone who can make you smile,
Even in the worst of times,
Someone to assist you,
In your most innocent crimes.
Someone to make you feel good,
When you're so unconfident,
Someone who's always there,
To keep and not just for rent.
Someone who always looks good,
But always tells you that you look better,
Someone who will let you borrow their clothes,
Because she's a trendsetter.
Someone who loves you,
Even when you're mean,
Someone who understands you,
And reminds you that you're only a teen.
Someone who has a great shoulder,
For you to come cry on,
Someone who may get mad,
But will always stay calm.
Someone who is real,
Our friendship, I will always see,
Someone who knows who I am,
This person is my best friend, Emily.

As Time Goes By
By Robyn Kroswek

Hush little baby, listen to my lullaby,
Life gets harder as time goes by.
Trust is not an issue, when you're lying in bed,
Simple little thoughts are running through your head.
So sweet and so pure, your bottle is in your hand,
Little diapers, little clothing, can't even stand.

Hush little baby, it's the first day of school,
Different times mean different rules.
Not so many worries and not so many fears,
Different reasons to cry your tears.
Time starts to fly, climbing up the grades,
Soon your childhood begins to fade.

Hush little baby, your teenage years, at this point, are closer,
Those simple little thoughts are now over.
You will start to grow up,
From little bows and dresses to perfume and make-up.
You will make choices to block out the hurt,
Probably wish that you were someone you weren't.

Hush little baby, soon you'll be an adult,
That's when things get difficult.
Then you'll make decisions on your own,
You make choices when you're grown.
You have no idea what's in store,
Sleep for now, I'll say no more.
Hush little baby, make the good times last,
Life gets harder as time goes past.

Clumsy

By: Olivia Lair

Whoops, sorry!
Oh geez, pardon me,
I'm not very good at keeping my balance.
Wherever I go, there is a chance,
that I'll probably end up on the floor.
Down the stairs and out the door,
I'm always coming back for more.
Yes, I know I slip and I fall,
all the time I trip and I stall.
Every time I still pick myself up,
And quickly wipe off my butt.
I just keep going,
no matter what!
Even at the movies I can't stand up straight,
I know I'm what gravity hates.
And if you surprise me,
or sneak up behind me…
Certainly I'll end up on the ground,
with a screaming sound.
And, oh, about the stairs,
They're giving me nightmares!
I'm minding my own business,
when in a moment of distress,
I fall on my bum.
So call me crazy,
But I think that just maybe
I am who I am
And that's clumsy!

Magnum XL-200, The Hypercoaster
By Cory Larmon.

A little over 20 years ago, Cedar Point, the Amazement Park, pulled off something amazing: The Magnum XL-200. At over 200 feet tall and almost a mile long, this roller coaster defined a new era. It was a record breaking behemoth of height and speed- only something the coaster capital of the world can rightfully make. Not many people seem to know, but the red terror known as the Magnum saved roller coasters as we know them.

During the 1980's as technology was improving as rapidly as ever with marvels such as the cell phone and game boy, people started to view those old, creaky, roller coasters as a thing of the past. So they turned to newer, more advanced ways of getting thrills such as 4D theaters and simulators which are basically rooms full of chairs that jerk around in front of a giant screen. In my opinion, that doesn't even come close to touching the sheer awesomeness of flying around on a high speed, heart racing thrill ride. When people heard of the gleaming, steel, amazement that was the magnum, they were utterly mesmerized to the point of knowing one thing: roller coasters were back. Thousands of visitors flocked to cedar point to see and ride the Magnum XL-200. The Magnum didn't just catch the attention of coaster fans but also the attention of competition. The race was on to design and create a new record breaker, some coasters did, but once again cedar point came out on top with the millennium force and later with the top thrill dragster. None of this would have happened without the help of the world's first hypercoaster, the Magnum XL-200. Now that you have the history, how about a ride from someone who has the experience?

After HOURS of waiting for the darned thing I finally hopped into my seat on the 20 year old history maker. Before I went, the thrill was delayed by an annoying coaster operator who tells me about the ride. I mean HELLO?! I am sitting right in front of the freaking thing! Well, once I was finally done listening to that, I was lurched forward to my inevitable doom- I mean awesome thrill ride! I seemed to float over the path other people are walking on in my very own retro style 80's spaceship. All of the sudden, the relaxation is over and I took a sharp right and started my trip up the first hill…gulp. The coaster moves S-L-O-W-L-Y up the man- made mountain of steel. I look to my right and see the Gemini, the record holder previous to the magnum and wonder how the heck people were okay riding THAT wimp. Before I knew it, I was at the tip-top, 205 feet in the atmosphere. They say you can see Canada, the great land of hockey, ice fishing, and saying "Eh" a lot from the top, but my attention was mainly focused on the 200 foot drop I was hanging over. AAAAAAAAAAAHHHHHHHHHHHH!!!!!!!!!!!!!!!! I plunged 200 feet toward the earth at speeds of 72 miles per hour!!! I had enough heights for one day but it was tough luck for me because I instantly headed up the 157 foot tall second hill! I rocketed down into the first tunnel which honestly isn't that great unless you ride through it at night! Well once I was out of that, I headed toward 2 horizontal loops that almost looked like a ribbon, but I knew THIS ribbon wasn't for tying to your dog's collar. I felt the centripetal force press down on my body as I traversed these wicked metal whip lashers and looked at the sand several feet below me.

Now for the trip back to the boarding station! It's a bumpy ride chock full of those awesome bumps known as airtime hills. Every time I hit one, I put my hands into the air for a few nanoseconds of sheer weightlessness and regretlessly forced myself through the sobering bump that followed. There are a couple tunnels with lights in them and in both of them, I experienced an abrupt drop. Once I finished, I hovered over that same walkway I was on a few minutes before and head straight to the boarding station. "How was your ride?" The coaster operator asks. I couldn't help but whooping out in delight. She says something about exiting the ride and having a great day at Cedar Point, the coaster capital of the world!

Slavery
By: Stephanie Leonard

Tragedy, Misery, Horrible,
> Wishes to stop.
Dreams of being free,
> Wants to be with family.
Who wonder's what it's like to be free?
> Enslaved children.
Who fears getting beaten?
> Slaves.
Who is afraid of slave owners?
> Slave traders.
Who would like to be with family?
> Who believes they will be free?
Who loves slavery?
> No one.
Who wants slavery?
> Southerners.
Who needs slavery?
> Cotton farmers.
Who plans to stop slavery?
> Whose final destination is freedom?

ALASKA!
By Bailey Liedel

Alaska is not what it seems,
Winter
freezing temperatures and snow filling the air.
Spring
beautiful flowers blossoming, like a dream.

Alaska is not what it seems,
Oceans
splash of frozen water,
unexpected swarms of lively otters.
the blue ocean view all around you.

Alaska is not what it seems,
Mountains
lovely views from the peaks looking down
like you are the queen of these grounds.
the snow white and fluffy lying on the peaks.

Alaska is not what it seems,
extended plane rides
paid off, all of it together is not a rip-off.
can't stay forever,
next time, bring your cozy sweaters!
Alaska is not what it seems.

Heaven

By Justin Lowry

In the year 2009
I went to Cooperstown New York.
In the car were my mom and dad
The longest car ride ever!

My heart started to pound
I was excited to get in the park.
I looked at all the other kids
Dying to play.

4 coaches and 12 players
We played a West Virginia team.
After our first game I say,
"This is like heaven, I wish I never had to leave. "

Zoey
By Nick MacInnes

For the longest time my mother had always wanted a Yorkshire Terrior. When our old poodle died this past summer, my Mom begged Dad for a new family dog. Mom searched the papers and made a few phone calls. Then on Thursday, August 13 around 4 or 5 pm, my family and I hopped in the car and left to go to Eaton Rapids. About two hours later, we arrived at a little farm house that was across the street from an old, rusty, red barn nestled in the middle of a large corn field. We got out of the car and went in to see the new little Yorkie puppies. We were surprised to see five adorable, bouncing little puppies. They all licked us, jumped on us and played with us. One, named Zoey, was really cute and she weighed about 2 pounds. Both parents of the puppies were there. Her dad was about the same size as Zoey and weighed 3 pounds, his name was "Chaz," and he was gray and black. "Lexi," Zoey's mother, weighed about 8 pounds. Sadly, Lexi was really a yappy dog and my Dad didn't want a yapper. She was gray and brown.

There was also another mother there, Zoey's Aunt, named "Mandi." Mandi was really quiet and was a really cool brownish red color, however, Yorkies are usually black and brown. There was another puppy we wanted, his name was Kodi and he was one of Mandi's puppys. According to my mom she said, "he was really spunky." He had his ears up high and was prancing all around, interested in everything. Choosing from these puppies wouldn't be easy and my Dad really didn't want a dog at all. Dad made us go home and think about it.

The next night Mom begged Dad to take us back and after giving my Dad "the sad puppy dog eye treatment" and lots of begging, we got Zoey because Kodi was already taken and the night before she took a nap in both my sister's and my lap. That night when we brought her home she slept in my mom's lap in the car all the way home. When we got home Zoey was full of energy and ready to play. We wore her out and she slept all night. I think she's the perfect dog because she doesn't bark that much and she doesn't bite.

Words of Lies
By: Valerie Magri

You said you wouldn't leave,
yet you walked out the door.
you come and you go like,
that's never happened before?

Come to you with open arms?
Sorry I can't do that!
I sit and I listen,
trying to hold back the tears.

You rage and you rant,
"Don't call me dad!"
"You're a selfish brat!"
"You're not my daughter!"

You think saying, "I'm sorry"
will make it all go away.
You want to pretend that
things aren't as bad as they were before.

I'm just a "responsibility"
That you said you didn't want.
The one you left here
to shed these tears.
I'm waiting and wishing
For you to come home,
to hear that you will never leave,
That this has all been a bad dream.

That day never happened,
mom said it wasn't anyone's fault.
You were here only to visit,
We would never be a family again.

I will blame myself forever,

for being so different.
For being such a burden,
that I pushed you away.

I know you don't love me
I know you never have.
Don't sit here and say you do,
those words mean nothing coming from you!

Do you remember?
By Alisha Mahaffey

Do you remember the times we spent together, the games we played?
And the toys we played with?
Do you remember how we always dressed up like we were older?
Do you remember all the songs we sung? And the dances we made up?
Do you remember the good times? Do you remember the bad?
Do you remember the fights we had? The horses we rode?
Do you remember the secrets we shared, and the stories we told?
Do you remember the school we went to, the teachers we had?
Do you remember the ice cream trucks we chased?
The parks we went to, the slushies we made?
Do you remember how sick it made me?
Do you remember how you never wanted me to leave?
Can you remember all the memories we have? I know I can.
Do you remember how sick you got?
Do you remember how sad I got?
Do you remember the clock on the wall and it just seems to tick your life
away until you had none?
But most of all do you remember me?
Do you know how hard it was to see a best friend in the ground?
Or how hard it was to see you each day and know that each day is one day
closer till the end?
Did you know that when you left, how many people missed you or how
many people cried?
Or how many people were hurt?
Did you know that I never wanted you to leave? Do you know how many
walks I took to help find the cure?
Do you remember the last time I saw you?
Do you know how long ago that was?
Do you know how much I miss you? Do you know that you shouldn't have left?
But I guess God wanted to be mean and take you away from everyone who
cared about you,
so he can have you all to himself.
God can be a selfish person sometimes Karly,
but when you stop and think about it,
Maybe he was doing it for the best
RIP

I Don't Know What to Do
By Shantanique McDonald

I never felt so sad since you left ,
my heart has been sore.
I cry to myself everyday
thinking why couldn't you stay.

Sleepless days restless nights,
I should have never let you out my sight.
Your love was so bright,
just a light.

My heart feels like dirt
I'm so very hurt.
I write poems about you everyday,
because I loved you in every possible way.

I don't know what to do,
all I know is I'm missing you.
I'm telling you this is all true
you were my boo!

What am I suppose to do?
Now that I lost you,
my heart is feeling so blue -
because I don't know what to do.

I just need you back
my life has been a wreck .
I have no clue what to do
my heart is feeling like a flu.

There's reasons why I cry
because I'm missing you -no lie,
I try to let you go
but it's very hard I'm telling you so.

I even wrote a song

about you!
Baby come back to me,
I'm missing you as you can see.

I need you in my life
without you its not right
I need you by my side
all day and all night.

When I was with you I felt so special
I felt like a princess in a castle.
Baby I don't know what to do
I'm officially missing you.

You made me feel like I was on top of the world
when you told me I was your favorite girl.
I loved you with all my heart
I hate that we are apart.

You was my favorite boy
every time I seen you my heart filled with joy.
I will never be the same without you
my heart is filled with pain.

I cry my eyes out everyday
wishing you was here to stay.
Every night my pillow gets soaked with tears
because losing you was not my fear

I don't know what to do
I really do miss you.
I thought I could move on
I guess I was wrong.

I wish that you loved me the way I loved you
I really don't know what to do.
I wish you would come back to me baby
come back home where you belong

I will hold on to our love
and make it strong .

I loved you with all I had
I'm sad and mad that you hurt me so bad.

I loved you with all my heart
I hate that we are apart.
I'm dangerously in love with you
I don't know what to do.

I wish we was still together
I love you now and forever.

Tyler
By: Kayla Middleton

Tyler is just a pain,
Tyler is always hurting someone,
They were all outside in Gram's backyard,
They were playing basketball.
Tyler passed the ball to Jacob,
But hit him right where it hurts!.
Tyler.
Tyler is always hurting someone,
Tyler is just a pain,
Tyler likes to play.
Mom and Tyler were in the living room
They were watching TV
Tyler went to stretch,
But hit mom in the face.
Tyler.
Tyler likes to play,
Tyler loves soccer,
Tyler is always hurting someone.
Tyler and my sister were out side,
They were playing soccer,
Tyler went to pass the ball to my sister,
But the ball hit her in the gut.
Tyler.
Tyler loves soccer,
Tyler breaks things,
Tyler is just a pain,
Tyler was outside,
Tyler was just kicking the ball around.
Tyler kicked the ball,
But it hit the window and broke it to a shatter,
Tyler.
Tyler is just a pain.

The Pain I'll Never Forget
By Tiffany Mountian

It was April 29, 2007. I was at my friend Alexis house, I woke up feeling horrible! The right side of my stomach was throbbing! I couldn't handle it, I wanted to burst out crying but I didn't want Alexis to be worried, so I did my best not to. Alexis looked at me with concern; she asked if I was okay. I responded saying I was fine, but inside I wasn't.

We ended up going to the park right after that. We where swinging, Running, Jumping, and laughing. It was so much fun; I kind of forgot about my side and had some fun. When we were leaving, I remember me and Alexis really wanted ice cream. We begged until her mom finally took us. I got a plain vanilla cone with sprinkles. We ate our ice cream on the way back to her house where my dad would be ready to pick me up.

As I was eating, the side pain came back. It was kicking in good! Alexis noticed I didn't seem okay again, before she could ask, I said "Alexis I don't feel good" she said "It's okay, I hope you feel better "We sat there and talked until we finally came up to a familiar house with my dads car parked on the side of the road. Alexis and I ran inside, I grabbed my stuff and we said our goodbyes.

I ran into my car, great that wasn't a smart move now my side started to hurt more. When I got in I told my dad how my side was killing me! But I didn't know it could literally kill me. He told me when we got home to tell my mom, see my mom works at the hospital so if it's something she has saw before she might know how to make the pain go away. I hoped it would all end soon.

We pulled up to the house and a walked inside the first thing I said was "Mom My side is killing me please help!" She walked over not so eager and said "Use your hand and show me where" I took my hand and placed it on the same spot it has been hurting all day. As I did her eye's got big and I could see worry in them. Then she started to speak, "Honey, I think it's your Appendix, if it is, you will need emergency surgery." I started to freak out, my mom tried to calm me down, she said to go to school tomorrow and if it still hurt call her as soon as possible. So I went to bed and fell asleep.

Before I knew it, the time came to get dressed and ready for school. My side wasn't feeling better at all. After about 20 minutes of getting ready, it was time to head to school. My mom drove me to school, I told her I felt okay, that was a lie. She dropped me off and I headed for my locker. I managed to stay calm until lunch time came. I got my usually hot lunch and headed to sit with my two best friends Taylor DeRousse and Taylor Warner.

Lunch has always been fun for me. We ate, laughed, and just talked. Then the time for us to go outside came. My side wasn't doing to well. We ran outside and went to play soccer with some of our other friends. As we where running the pain hurt more then ever, I just couldn't take it. I stopped and sat by this really big tree. Taylor D and Taylor W came running over to me. They saw I was crying. Taylor D asked why I was crying, and I told her everything about my side, and how I needed to get to the office to go home. Taylor, being as nice as she always is walked me up to the office to miss playing soccer.

When I walked up to the front of the desk the lady there asked me what she could help me with. I told her how my side hurt and it might be my Appendix, so if it got worse my mom wanted me to call home as soon as possible. Right away this lady gave me a disgusting look as if I made all this up and just wanted to get a day   off of school. I hate when people think your lying.

She ended up letting me call home, I told my mom it was getting worse, she said she would be there right away. I got a pass to go to my locker to get my things and tell my teacher and friends I'm leaving and goodbye. When I got to the office, my mom was there and she said we where ready to go. She signed me out and we where off.

As I hopped into the car she told me she made an appointment for me to get a CAT scan. We drove in silence I was just to sore and tired to talk, thinking to myself I hopped this would end soon. As we got to the doctors, I started to get nervous. We walked into the doctors and headed to the elevator because the room I needed to go to was in the underground floor. My mom knew exactly where to go, I followed her until we reached a room that was all white and sort of quite.

My mom had me sit down as she walked to the front desk to talk to the lady. My mom came back with three cups of something that looked kind of like lemonade. She handed me one of the cups and told me I had to drink all three. It was a special dye I had to drink that would make everything on the inside of my body light up in the CAT scan pictures. The "lemonade" was not good at all, but at least they put in an effort to make it not so gross.

After waiting for about 15 minutes, it was time to get the CAT scan. The doctor called my name and we headed for a room, with a needle on a plate and a big machine. I'm guessing that was the CAT scan. They had me sit on a weird metal board. The doctor grabbed my arm and told me to be very still. I did as she told me. The stuff in the needle she was putting in my arm was another dye to help see different things in my body. The needle didn't hurt to bad, but the dyes in it, made me feel kind of cold.

The metal board I was laying on started to move into the scan, the doctor told me to hold my breath for 10 seconds, so I did. I had to do that about 3 times. The CAT scan was pretty fast, and it wasn't as bad as I thought it would be. The doctor took my mom to a back room that you could see the pictures the scan took. By the way she was shaking her head; I was guessing I would have surgery soon. My mom came out, with the news I expected. It was my appendix and we had to get home fast to get my clothes and my dad so we could head over to the hospital.

I tried my best to not cry until we reached the car. Right when we got it, I burst out crying. The whole car ride I just cried, and cried and cried. When we got to the house my mom went and grabbed my clothes as my dad got in the passenger's seat. He said everything was going to be fine, but I didn't think I was. My mom came out super fast and got into the car. Then we were off.

My side was hurting more than ever, after about 15 minutes of driving, we where almost there, but the bumps we where hitting we so painful I screamed. My dad turned around and said we where almost there and not to be worried. 5 minutes after that we pulled up to the hospital, we had the man there take our car to the garage as my mom took me to a room where I would prepare for surgery. The nurse came in and had the I-V All ready for me. Man did I hate getting I-V's put in. It's dreadful.

It took the nurse 6 attempts until she finally got the needle in a vain. I sat down as the nurse gave me a medicine that made me sort of go crazy. I didn't remember this much, but my parents are always talking about how after they gave me that medication I started screaming, "Mom hold my head, it's moving mom please hold my head!" The thing was, my head was perfectly still.

After a few minutes, I remember being pulled onto an operation table, the last thing I remember before going out was seeing the knives they where going to be cutting me with, great that's exactly what I wanted to see. A man, I'm guessing one of the nurses tapping on my head saying "hang in there peanut," Then BOOM. I was out.

I woke up in a hospital room on a bed with my parents hovering over me. They asked how I was feeling, I said fine, this time I was telling the truth. Being at the hospital was so boring, I mean all I did was sleep and eat, then sleep more. My aunt, cousin and grandparents stopped by to see me, it was nice seeing how concerned they all where. I was super happy to get cards, toys, even a gorilla stuff animal I ended up calling appendicitis, because I had my appendix removed.

After a wait of two days, it was finally time for me to return to my favorite place, home. I remember being so happy. It was Wednesday May 2, three more days until my birthday. A man at the hospital came in my room and said, "You ready to go." All I did was hope out of bed, but instead of just walking to the car, the guy there said I probably shouldn't walk much so he pushed me in a wheel chair with my mom strolling behind us. We got to the front of the car and I hoped right in there and sat next to my sister, who was being quit nice lately. Then we where ready to head home. This time, I could actually ride in a car without complaining how bad my side hurt. As we were driving my parents asked what the staples felt like where my scar was. I didn't really feel them.

We pulled up to our house; I hopped out and headed for my room very slowly. I got on my bed with my sister and we watched T.V. Later that day Taylor DeRousse came over, when she walked in her mom told me I walked like an old lady. I thought it was funny. she brought me an envelope full of cards from everybody at school, most of them said they missed me and couldn't wait until I came back to school. Taylor and I read them all. Before we knew it Taylor had to get going so we said our goodbyes. The rest of the day I spent time with the family, me and my older sister had a lot of fun actually talking and not fighting.

That was the year I felt one of the worst pain I have ever felt. I would never wish anybody to have there appendix removed, It's a painful process but I was really happy once it was over. Have you ever had a surgery or something removed?

By Andrew Movahedan

Basketball
Run, Shoot
Dribbling, Running, Sweating
Pistons, Lakers, Magic, Warriors
Life, Competitive, Exciting
Fun, Relaxing
Life

Rules
Moves, passes
Shooting, Fouling, Referees
Bulls, Mavericks, Clippers, Jazz
Exhausting, extreme, sweating
Jumping, Hot
Accomplished

Favorite sport
Adrenaline, intense
Shooting, traveling, charging
Rockets, Suns, Cavaliers, Nets
Arguing, Fighting, Frustrated
Jump, shoot
Dunking

Tornado Alley

By: Sofia Navarro

It was the last soccer game of the season, and we were facing the hardest team, other than us. It was getting cloudy and looked like it was going to rain, but we loved the rain and didn't care. By the second half, we were tied, and the ref said we had about five minutes to go, so we played hard. One of our best players finally got the ball and bolted up the field with it and scored the winning goal. We congratulated the other team and were heading out for our awards ceremony and party at the bowling alley and to make pizzas.

When we got to the bowling alley, it was starting to rain and the wind was picking up. When I got there, not all the players were there, so we decided to start playing hide and seek; the clouds made the room darker inside so it was a lot more fun. We were waiting for about ten minutes until everyone arrived, and we were ready to start making pizzas. They took about an hour to get all 13 girls pizza's ready and we were starving. We served our parents first, of course, and then stuffed our faces with food. Then, the lights started flickering, and then they went out, and we heard the sirens. Everyone ran to the windows, to see the amazing sight of trees uprooting, power lines flying, and the rain shooting past us. Then, we heard a loud crash and a bright blue flash. A tornado was coming.

You would think that hearing the loud wind and thunder would scare everybody, but instead of everyone freaking out like you would think; we were playing capture the salt and pepper shaker (capture the flag). After about 20 minutes the tornado was gone and sirens stopped. One of the girl's dads's said that the flash was because lightning hit a tree branch, and it fell and hit a power line, and it blew out. After a few minutes of hoping that the power would come back on, we decided to go outside when the rain was stopping to get our trophies and pictures. That was the best awards ceremony we ever had and definitely, the most memorable.

The Ocean
By: Becca Neal

I walk the ocean, Daytona Beach, watching the wave's crash ashore. Coarse, soft sand attached to my feet. I rest there, enjoying scorching in the hot sun, my winter chills to my dry skin.

I look out into the distance watching dolphin's leap in and out of the rough, blue water. While Jelly fish lie everywhere stuck to the wet sand, as kids glide over them.

I look down, at the clear blue water as textured shells wash up in the mucky sand. The water giving me the chills, I soon turn back to my towel, sand kicking behind me, hoping to get a suntan.

I lay there on a soft towel with the shifting ground beneath, the sun beaming right on me. My eyes glazed at kids building sand castles that collapse after many attempts, teenagers playing any and every sport there is not watching who they might hit next and adults flying their kid's kites perfectly swaying in the sky. Although these many activities look amusing, I still don't have the strength to pick my lazy self up.

I see far out, surfers out in the distance riding each wave, as they effortlessly skid across the salt water. I feel sand hitting my back, from the cars tires brushing against the sand, which are driving 10 mph to see the prominent site. It sure is Daytona Beach, one of the only beaches that allow cars to drive on the beach.

I slowly pick myself up off my towel, making my way up the beach for lunch to the scent of smoke from the grill floating through the air, I suddenly halt. I catch a glimpse of a figure sticking out of the sand; I stop to pick it up. I had in my hand, gleaming in the sun a full sand dollar, a great treasure.

I sprint down the stairs, reaching the ocean, after a delicious meal. Standing their looking down the beach at all the people and up in the sky at the flocks of birds. Thinking to myself what the day will be like when I have to leave behind the beautiful weather and ocean, to return back where I belong.

A Soccer Balls lifestyle
By Conor Nolan

Here I am, sitting in the darkness,
Hatching up a master plan to escape,

Then suddenly, a crack of light appears,
I'm pulled out of the bag with some tape,

With bad thoughts in my head, and lines on me painted red,
Wondering why these weird humans chose me,

I can see in my sight, a flabby arm gripped tight,
And can hear him speaking loudly,

Finally I'm dropped, into a sea of green,
Confident, I try to hop away,

A player uses his cleat, being very neat,
As he insures that I will stay,

The ref blows his whistle, fast as a missle,
As the players get in their positions,

Two people by me, looking very, very nasty,
Like they're in great condition,

Here we go; one kicks me with his toe,
Looks like this game is about to start,

I see all the kids run, it looks pretty fun,
Don't they know I'm just bought from wall-mart?

I soar through the air, knowing only to prepare,
As the goalie dives to make a sweet save,

Slipity slopity, flipity flopity,
Getting treated like I am some slave,

I get blown by the air, bounce off a chair,
As the goalie punts me off the dome,

Like a lion from a den, or a pig from a pen,
I really just want to get home.

Nail In My Foot
By Michael Norman

When I was 12, at my old house, I was playing with my brother and sister and a friend of theirs. My mom was at work and we had a baby sitter watching us. For some reason we had a tree that used to have a clubhouse in it and the tree still had a couple of pieces of wood in it. One piece of wood with a nail in it was sticking straight up and I climbed the tree for fun. When I was getting down I jumped right on that piece of wood and the rusty nail went right through my foot. At first I thought it just went through my shoe, so I tried to pull it out but it went right into my foot and it hurt so much it felt like 1000 needles going through my foot I was crying and screaming a lot.

So I tried to walk back to my house but it hurt too much to walk, so I fell to the ground and told my brother and sister to go and get the baby sitter, and then I sat there and waited. The babysitter came and picked me up and tried to walk into the house but the piece of wood kept shaking. It hurt too much so I told her to stop and put me down on the ground. She called 911 and then we waited for them to come. They showed up calmed me down and then they grabbed the piece of wood and ripped it out of my foot so they could get off my shoe it felt like a hammer hitting my foot it, hurt so much. They looked at the wound, and it was gushing blood and it shot like five inches, so they put some bandages on it to stop the gushing blood. I asked them not to take me to the hospital in an ambulance, so the babysitter called my mom. She was at work so she called my grandmother. My older sister didn't even know what happened until someone told her about it. She was probably watching TV downstairs.

My grandma showed up and took me to the hospital. I called a couple of my friends and told them about it. When we got to the hospital, it smelled like floor cleaner and what ever else it smells like. They had us sit in the waiting room until my mom got there and we answered a few questions. After that, they took me to the x-ray room and took x-rays of my foot. They found out there were a couple of pieces of the rust in my foot and the nail just barely missed plunging into my bone marrow. I had to soak my foot in soapy hot water and I had to get a tetanus shot in my arm for the rust. I saw a friend of mine there, which was cool. The funny thing is they were there for a foot check-up too!

When I was finally done I went to my grandma's house. That was a good thing that happened to me. The bad part was I had to soak my foot everyday in soapy hot water and take giant pills that were the size of grapes I had to walk with a cane for the whole time I was at my grandma's house. The tetanus shot I got for the rust hurt real bad for two days straight I couldn't even sleep on my arm. It was all really bad, but another good part was that I got to skip school for a week. The best part was it was right before spring break, so I got to stay at my grandma's house for two weeks.

The Struggle
By: Jimmy Olerich

For all the pain and hurt I got
For how I always play a lot
For all the things that I went through
For all the practice that I do
For today our playoffs start
For how I hope we don't fall apart
For now we are in the fall
For how we're still playing baseball
For how baseball is my best sport
Probably because all my support.

The Feel
By: Jimmy Olerich
Baseball has a lot of pain
But without pain there would be no gain
Baseball is a never ending game
The games are all different, never the same
Because there is no better feeling
Then getting a base hit then stealing
Winning is what I want to do
Try my hardest, I got to
Cause its baseball.

GRANDPA
by :Jacob Plautz

I wake up wondering, when will it be his time to go? He is already 64, how long will he be able to hold on? I spend as much time as possible with him just in case he does pass soon. So far we have found that he has a small amount of cancer. He also just recently had a long, teeth clenching process done on his knee. He was healing in the hospital, a frightening thing had happened. He was walking to the bathroom, he stumbled on some long, heavy cords that were hooked up to his blood pressure scanner, he fell to his knees and the stitches holding the open flesh wound closed burst. Suddenly blood and anti-bacterial juice poured out onto the floor and formed a orange liquid mess. (It was orange because of the thick blood and the yellow anti bacterial medicine.) After the devastating event, he was now hospitalized for five more days. We visited him for several days while he was in there, Finally he got to come home. It was such a relief to see him back on the couch.

Ever since I was born, my grandpa and I have had a special relationship. When I started to get older he took me fishing in his boat that we named "Blue By U." We got up early in the morning and grabbed our tackle boxes and hit the lake for about five hours. Even if we didn't have the smell on our hands, it was always a great time fishing with grandpa. On rainy days, we would stay in and play chess with his old time chess set. The smell of old wood and dust filled my nose when we opened the case. He desperately tried to teach me, but I still do not know what to do. The best part though was him still tried to teach me. When I grow up I want to be a loving, caring, father and grandfather just like him.

My little cousins, Zac and Ian, love to hang with my grandpa too. They always like to help him out with the little things around the house and garage. When my grandpa is out in the garage, us boys hop onto our loud dirt bikes and quads, which smell like exhaust, and drive on over to see which project we would be working on with him. It could be anything from working on his 4x4 quad to just sitting around messing with spare wood. When my grandpa is gone, I will have a piece of me missing, a giant black hole in my life.

I go to him for advice about life and my sports, when I get so mad, or if in trouble I go there to sleep it off and just to talk about it. All of that will be gone when he has passes. Zac and Ian will feel the same because they share a close relationship with him too. Life is the key to happiness and he is the life and happiness I never want to leave. Thinking about losing him is very painful. I love him very much, more than anyone will ever know. For now we have to enjoy the time we have and keep doing more amazing things every day to ensure that life will always be better. When people say they have a special person to tell every little thing to, or spill out their true feelings about something or someone I know for me it's my grandpa.

The Battle Within
by Bradley Olewinski

I felt power, like I was in control. I could do anything I wanted and nothing could stop me! A group of five or six warriors line up in front of me. They didn't stand a chance as they were decimated by my sword. As I turned around I was impaled in the shoulder by a sword. In a sudden rage I turned around trying to kill the man that just injured me. With the sword still in my shoulder, I gripped the man by his neck and slowly squeezed. I threw his lifeless body aside. I tried to walk but failed miserably and fell down into nothingness.

I woke up panting, wondering about the vivid dream that just flashed before my eyes. I got out of my bed and examined the room; not remembering exactly where I was. I felt the ship rock and there were sirens going off. Not thinking much about it, probably just was a training exercise, which I always seem to miss. The commander of this ship assured us no one knew we were here. The commander also said that we could be more carefree. I walked to the side of my bed to get my equipment. I went to the bathroom to change and glanced at myself. I was still standing tall at 6'1" while my brown hair was down to the top of my eyebrows. My hair really needed to be cut soon. My body used speed more than anything else. I don't trust anyone and I tend to be harsher than anyone else on the ship. When I was done putting on my armor I began thinking about my past as a soldier.

I was an experienced combatant. Nothing fancy, just a regular who fought in the Galactic War for three years. The Galactic war was between The Galactic Defenders of the Universe and Chaos Factions. The 'Chaosics' are what we called the Chaos Factions. They were an evil society made up of basic criminals. Soon the basic criminals became powerful warriors and expert marksman. They were trained and with time they had increased in numbers. Their weapons were usually a modified sword, made up of parts they found. The designs of their swords became a legendary trademark and were named Chaos Blades. They also had energy rifles that were able to shoot through most armor, although they would get jammed or overheated fairly easy but they were still a force to be reckoned with. The Chaosics would use unorthodox ways to kill a captured warrior and would annihilate any person in order to get what they wanted.

The Galactic Defenders of the Universe soon got the name 'GDU'. They are elite warriors trained to defend the people. Their swordsmanship is the greatest in the galaxy; they could at least match three Chaosics in battle. They were not as powerful marksman as the Chaosics but usually charged straight into a fight. While they had power and skill the Chaosics had numbers and cunning strategies. The GDU were almost defeated and had been pushed back to the inner worlds by the Chaosics. However a Galactic Spartan became a leader and the tides were about to change.

The Galactic Spartans were the GDU's special infantry. They were able to use special abilities such as heal a massive amount of troops, use lightning to strike their opponents, slow down time and much more. They wore a bright white armor that glowed in the sun. They also might wear a white cape for more movement if they need that extra speed because it was lighter. They carried around a Light Sword. The Light Swords were full of energy and could strike through even the greatest of armor. The Spartans travel in pairs, master and apprentice. The downfall to this new breed of soldiers is that their numbers are few and The Supreme Council never let Spartans fight in the war. They thought it was too 'dangerous.'

The Spartan arrived as the GDU were assembling their forces for one last attempt to defeat the Chaosics. He was an expert in battle tactics. His name was Seleas, his apprentice was Sion. Seleas used everything to win. He would leave worlds unprotected to strengthen others. He was more strategic than regular generals; he would spare no one and do anything to defeat his enemy. This brings me to the final battle, the battle of Izor V. Izor V was a planet not colonized. This would be the Chaosics' final push. Seleas had all of his ships positioned in a sneak attack. As one part of the fleet retreated the other part of the fleet would strike the main fleet, for a quick victory. Boy was he wrong! As his fleet retreated, Seleas saw the entire force of the Chaosics. He expected there to be about 50 ships. There were thousands of Chaosic ships. He planned accordingly and on each of the retreating ships there was a nuclear bomb. He said that they were coming to help the retreating ship, but they were really retreating themselves. He typed in the code and hit the activate button. The result left no Chaosics ships but half of his fleet was gone.

When Sion saw his master again he noticed that his master had changed. He seemed darker and guilt was the only thing his eyes showed. His eyes were also red as if he had been crying and his face was pale. He told the remaining ships to go to Otez Prime and no one saw Seleas again or at least not the one they all remembered.

Years later, Seleas was a changed man and formed a new faction, The Resurrected or 'Res' for short. No one knew why, some think it was what he did, killing millions of people in the final battle. Others thought he was always evil just waiting for the right to show his true way. Seleas's apprentice Sion, joined the Resurrected and so did the rest of the fleet. The two Spartans became the Dark Spartans and leaders of the Res. They changed their capes and armor to a pure black. Without light you probably couldn't see them even if they were right in front of you. Their Light Swords now became the Dark Swords. Instead of light energy flowing through them, Seleas infused dark energy with them. Their infantry numbers started at 300,000 which was pretty much the entire fleet.

When Seleas and Sion tried to find a planet for a base of operation, they were ambushed by a small resistance of Chaosics that happened to still be alive. Everything was going well until Seleas was attacked by a large group of Chaosics in an abandon building. Seleas fought and killed them all. As he was leaving he was gravely injured and never returned from that planet. No one knows what happened. Only Sion may have known, but he never spoke about it and continued his masters' work.

Five years later the Resurrected have over 50 million troops and 1,000 Dark Spartans controlling armies. The Dark Spartans now have more dark abilities then the GDU Spartans. They could destroy people's minds and suck the life force out of them, along with brutal ways of torture. The Res soldiers were great overall infantry, they could shoot at long distances, while still being able to fight in close combat. The Resurrected soldiers had black armor and the only way to tell their ranks apart were their emblems. The Res mostly attacked at night since you could hardly see them. The GDU soldiers could out fight them in close range but were outmatched in long range. The GDU Spartans also had to learn new powers to defend against these Dark Spartans. The GDU called them counter abilities. Sion declared war on the GDU and the war has continued on for two years. The GDU are once again pushed back to the inner worlds while the Res control all the outer and middle worlds.

I felt the ship shake again, shifting me out of my thoughts. I was about to go to the bridge to see the commander of the ship and demand to know what was going on when the door shot open. I pulled out my scatter blade, an effective blade that is very sharp and lightweight, tensing, waiting to strike and not knowing who it is. I breathed a sigh of relief. It was only a GDU soldier. He looked middle age, with a crew cut and dark brown hair. He had his normal armor on but seemed to be missing his helmet. He was one or two inches taller than me and looked stronger than me.

"Hey, I'm Brett, you're my bunk mate but since we have opposite shifts we kept missing each other," Brett said.

"Hi, my name's Bradley. What's going on?" I asked. I also asked myself how we never saw each other if we were in the exact same room?

"We got ambushed by a Resurrected ship. I have no clue how Sion found one of our main Spartans, Conor, who was on this ship. We have to make sure he made it to the escape pods." I examined Brett, he seemed shaken and his sword was gripped tightly like he was expecting a battle.

"What's so important about this one Spartan?" I asked. Not remembering who the Spartan was and I still didn't remember how I got on this ship, it rather concerned me.

"This one Spartan can turn the tides of battles. He can make one side more confident and the other side fatigued. He has helped the GDU win some crucial battles and he's one of a kind." He looked amazed; personally I would like to see him in action before I judged him.

"Let's see if Conor is already off the ship," I said. We went through the door and turned the corner to see a small firefight going on. There were two Res soldiers and only one GDU. The Res soldiers seem to have the upper hand and I was about to tell Brett a plan to surprise the intruders. Before I could say a word Brett decided to leap into action and yelled "Charge," at the top of his lungs.

I sighed, this is going to become a habit isn't it, thinking to myself? I pulled out my scatter blade and charged at the Res soldiers. One of them started to blind fire before I stabbed him in the gut. I pulled out my bloody blade to see that the other Res soldier was down and Brett was still standing. I kind of wish I had left him back in the room especially if he was going to keep risking our safety like that. The GDU soldier the Res was fighting died and I wish we could have had one more person in our squad. I was about to snap at Brett for doing something so stupid but decided against it. He was a recruit, or so I assumed. They do say actions speak louder than words.

We started to head to the next door when I felt a strange sensation overcome me. I felt like I knew what was happening behind the door. It seemed like a Light Spartan and a Dark Spartan were fighting behind the door, at least that's what I thought. Logic told me it must be Conor's apprentice because I was sure Conor would be the first one into the escape pods. I told Brett to search the bodies for anything useful before we headed off, giving whoever was behind that door some time to finish off one another. Brett gave me this disgusted look before he went off. Before Brett returned I went to open the door were the battle was occurring, thinking it must be over. As I did, I experienced an unknown pain. My vision started to blur and my head felt as if it were about to explode into a billion pieces. Before I blacked out I thought I heard Brett say something, but I wasn't sure.

The first thing I noticed was black everywhere. I looked down to see that my right hand was glowing white. I did a double take. Yep, it definitely was glowing. I became confused and I glanced at the rest of my body hoping that the glow was everywhere and perfectly normal. It wasn't. My arm was the only thing glowing in this dark and lonely place. I felt sudden pain in my left arm. The darkness around me started to engulf my left hand, the one that was not glowing. It felt like I was just placed over a fire. I screamed in agony as it continued to spread across my body, up my legs, through my chest, until it reached my right arm. It stopped, like it was a little kid that had stumbled across a door and couldn't get through. I felt the darkness going up my neck and the pain increasing. It soon hit my face. The lower part of my vision started to disappear. The last thing I remember before the lights went out was that my arm was still glowing but now it was red.

As my eyes shot opened I was instantly greeted by two pairs of eyes. Wait… two pairs of eyes? I tensed expecting some sort of brutal interrogation when I saw Brett looking at me with great concern. "What happened?" I asked, relived that I wasn't going to be tortured.

"Well after you told me to search the bodies," I noticed Brett was glaring at me, "you went to go check what was behind the door when I saw you collapse. I yelled your name and then Conor…" I looked over to the other person he was talking about, "burst through the door to see what the yelling was all about and saw us. He knew we were GDU and he helped me carry you to the escape pods. We got off the ship just as it exploded. The escape pod we were in landed inside this building. We got you in a bed as soon as possible. We heard you yelling so we came to check what was happening."

As Brett was talking I looked over at Conor. I took this chance to examine him. He looked 5'7" maybe. His hair was short and brown, yet his face stood out the most. He had two battle scars, one running from his left eye to his ear and the other across his right eye. His battle scars made him look old, but I believed him to only be about 27. I tried remembering what Brett said earlier about a 'special Spartan' because his name sounds familiar. Now I remember! This is Spartan Conor, he must have been fighting behind the door before I fainted. He's the one that can turn the tide of the battle. He looks way different than I thought he would. I hope he is as good as the stories say. I'll probably find out later.

I decided not judge him just yet. I slowly sat up, thinking about my dream. I glanced at my arm hoping it still wouldn't be glowing. It wasn't, thankfully. I asked Brett how long I was out, not caring about my hand at the moment. He said I was out for two days! I must have had a completely bewildered look on my face because he told me on the way down to the planet that I hit my head as we launched off in the escape pod.

I looked at Conor again he would constantly glance at my arm with a strange look in his eye. I figured something must have happened while I was 'dreaming' that only he could see. I followed his eyes to see that my arm was still perfectly fine and nothing seemed wrong. "So what do you know about this place *Conor*?" finishing with a distrusting tone. He heard this and looked away. He was hiding something! Possibly something important and he wouldn't tell us. Just let me get him alone and he will tell me! My eyes widened in shock wondering what came over me. I never knew I could be so harsh but luckily Conor didn't see my eyes widen because his eyes were focused completely on the wall to my left.

"I... th-think this pl-planet is uh... p-po-possibly Otez P-Prime," he shakily said.

"Conor, what's wrong?" Brett asked. He obviously didn't hear what I just said.

"N-nothing," Conor said, his voice still stuttering a little.

"Let's get going," I said as I started to put some less noticeable armor on. I wasn't sure if Otez Prime was controlled by the Res. We started to head out the door. As it opened I saw a fairly large hallway. This placed didn't seem so bad. "Hey, Conor do you know anything about this planet?" I asked him again because Brett was not the smartest person around.

"I-I heard a little about it, but I don't know it as well because it is a middle planet and we hardly ever leave the inner planets. I do know one thing about it though, it is a planet controlled by the Resurrected," he explained. I turned my head and gave Conor a 'you idiot' look.

"I would have liked to know that before we left the room, but thank goodness that I made us wear regular, black armor," I said as we walked along. I noticed that there was no one in this area of the building. It was also so quiet all you could hear was the noises our shoes made as they pressed into the ground. As we got to a corner I saw four Resurrected soldiers.

"Hey you, you're not suppose to uarghhhh..." I heard him groan as my sword went through his stomach and out the other side. I pulled my sword out with one smooth motion. The other three soldiers quickly reacted and started firing upon us. I glanced at my two allies to see Brett already charging and Conor pulling out his Light Sword. I returned my attention to the remaining three soldiers as I heard a shot wiz by my head. The next shot the soldier took connected with my chest. I grunted with pain but still continued forward. I watched Brett strike an opponent and heard a loud grunt assuming Brett finished him off for sure. Conor was currently locked in combat with a soldier. His arm was bleeding and I suspected he had gotten hit with a sword blow. I heard Conor yell something as I felt another shot hit my arm, almost making me drop my sword. I drew closer to my opponent and I saw him desperately try to get his sword out. His sword never left his hilt as he dropped to the floor, unmoving.

"Conor! Are you ok?" I asked him as I ran over to check his wounds. As I got over there to check his arm I saw a bright blue light engulf his arm.

"I'm fine, with these healing abilities I have I'm able to heal all minor cuts," he said as the light faded from his arm.

"That's amazing!" Brett exclaimed as he saw Conor heal himself. These

Spartans didn't really seem like the warriors in the great stories I heard about my younger years. This Spartan got hurt from a regular soldier. I thought they would have at least known how to handle a sword so they wouldn't get hurt. I looked at where I got shot. The bullets hadn't penetrated my armor but I was really going to feel some pain there later.

"Conor maybe you should stay behind us and use longer attacks, like your powers, so you don't get hurt." I told him. He actually listened to me. I would think a Spartan like him would be angry with my commands. Although I could tell he was afraid of me, like I could actually hurt him.

"Brett go scout out ahead to make sure we don't run into any more unwanted visitors," I said.

"Ok," he replied.

As soon as Brett got further down the hall I decided this would be the time I could asked Conor what he was hiding from us. "So Conor, why did you keep glancing at my arm when I woke up?" I asked him.

"I didn't keep glancing at your, what are you talking about?" he replied.

"I know what I'm talking about. You wouldn't look me in the eyes and you always looked at my arm as if it would kill you. You better tell me what your hiding or else!" I threatened. That seem to do the trick, his eyes widened and he took a step back.

"I'm n-not suppose t-t-to t-tell y-you," he said as his stuttering returned.

"You can tell me about this arm thing and what's got you so afraid of it," I told him as I thrust my 'special' arm at him, trying to get him to talk.

He leaped away from my arm, pulling out his sword and he yelled something I couldn't understand. Pain convulsed through my left arm. The pain spread through my body as I fell to my knees. I looked over to see Brett running with his weapon out, ready to attack Conor. I made a feeble attempt to tell Brett to stop, but he didn't hear me.

"What are you doing?" I heard Brett shout. Conor didn't answer as Brett flew against the wall. He struggled back up to his feet and tried to get to Conor but Conor lifted him up with his powers. He brought Brett closer, I tried to help but found I was stuck to the ground.

"Muhahahhahah," I heard Conor menacingly laugh. I took another look at Conor just long enough to find out he no longer looked like the Conor I first met. His appearance had changed entirely and didn't have scars running across his face. His head was bald and he had a face that had darkness written all over it. His once white Light Sword was now pure black and a black cape covered his body.

"My plan was already ruined but now I get to kill you again! The even better thing is you don't remember, Ahahahah!" Conor or whoever this guy was laughed out. What did he mean 'kill you again' and what don't I remember. Before I could ask, I heard a snap and Brett's body was on the ground, his head tilted sideways in an awkward position. Anger built up inside me as I let out a roar, but I still couldn't move.

"Well, why don't I tell you who you are before you die. You are Seleas! Ahahaha…" as I heard that my life flashed before my eyes.

I thought I 'died' in that abandon building after forming the faction the Resurrected. I was trying to find a base of operations and was ambushed by some Chaosic resistance. After I fought a pathetic group of Chaosics I remember being stabbed in the shoulder. I turned around and saw my apprentice, with the sword still in my back I picked him up by his neck and squeezed. I didn't say anything knowing he wanted my position as the leader of the Resurrected. I thought he was dead as I threw him aside. The pain in my shoulder was unbearable and as I tried to walk away I fell down, unmoving on the ground. I felt the sword in my shoulder pull out and I was ruthlessly flipped around. I saw my apprentice stand above me, raise his sword and finish me off. I was found later by a GDU scout and was returned to the Supreme Council. They healed my wounds but my memories were erased and for the safety of the GDU I was placed in a ship, far away from the inner worlds. They wanted to make sure I wouldn't remember anything that might return me as leader of the Resurrected.

Another memory flashed through my mind as I was digesting this information. *I remember a GDU Spartan training exercise. They were trying to get me angry. They had me in restraints and slowly hurt my friends to find the power I possessed. I remember breaking free of my restrains and my right arm had power flowing off of it in a dark red light. I killed the person who was torturing my best friend, as I smashed his head against the wall. The power I had was amazing as I lifted my friend, Brett, from his torture. I had known Brett since I was a child and we grew up as best friends. The Supreme Council sent me to the war because they thought I was too 'dangerous' to be there so close to them. Brett must have decided to come along. After I lost my memories he followed me hoping that I would get my memories back and remember faster with him there.*

Now I recognized who this man was standing in front of me. He was my apprentice. Sion must have disguised himself as Conor to try and sneak in to kill the council men of the Supreme Council. He didn't realize he infiltrated the ship that was sent to the outer worlds to see if my memories would come back. He must have found out that this ship wasn't going to return home for a while, so he contacted forces. I suspected that they couldn't get him off so they told him leave via the escape pods and would pick him up on the planet. On the way to the escape pod he must have found me and recognized me instantly. Sion at that time was out numbered and decided that he would wait until we were alone before reminding me who I once was. His plan worked and now he has just killed my best friend.

I suddenly charged at Sion, his eyes widened in shock. He didn't expect me to remember all my abilities as a Spartan and break whatever power was holding me to the ground. My right arm looked as if it were on fire as the power ran through my arm targeting him. Sion had a scared look in his eyes as he tried to defend against my onslaught as I brutally attacked him. His powers were useless as he tried to defend himself. I would use a counter ability to block each attack and strike with greater force each time he tried to push me away. In the end, I severely wounded Sion, he was now lying right next to my best friend hardly breathing.

"Hahaha… you…" he stopped for moment while he coughed, "you… think this… is over hahaha. My armies… are already… launching their… final attack… there is nothing… you can…do hahaha. One… more thing… die…" he finished as he took his last breath. I wondered what he meant when I saw a shadow out of the corner of my eye. I hardly felt any pain as a sword went through my shoulder. As I fell to the ground, my mind wandered as I was remembering who I've been, who I am and who I will become. Has my leadership come to an end or will I start anew?

GUITAR
By: Wade Panizzoli

Playing guitar is like my life, I would be doing absolutely nothing if I was not playing. I play it every chance I get to because it's amazing.

I received my first guitar from my parents in December of 2006. It was a First Act guitar, one of the worst guitar companies ever. My parents got me one of these guitars because they didn't know if I would like, or continue to play guitar so they got me a cheap one. I actually started to learn to play from guitar lessons at McCourt's music store in January of 2007. I have been continuing lessons till this year. I'm really thankful that my parents let me do this because they're rather expensive. $30 an hour for lessons and I do them once a week.

After a year of playing with that junky guitar, I told my parents that this guitar was a piece of trash, and that I've gotten good and think I should get a new one now. They said "I don't know", because they didn't want to spend the money. But on my birthday, they got me a guitar case, I said "oh cool thanks" in a disappointed way. "Open it up" they said. I then unzipped the case carefully and BOOM an Ltd Viper-50 was laying there. I was so surprised right then. At that moment I realized that I wanted to be serious about guitar.

Some people teach themselves how to play guitar, with help on the internet or they just learn how to play by ear. I was 10 or 11 at the time I started to play so I didn't know how to teach myself. Many famous guitarists learn how to teach themselves like Jimi Hendrix, Daron Malakian, Synyster Gates and a lot of other great guitarists. I wish I taught myself how to play kind of because I would have something to do all that time and it would be cool to tell people you learned on your own. Plus my parents would save a ton of cash.

My current guitar is a Fender Telecaster. I bought it at Motor City Guitar for around $230. I was debating on what guitar to get, so I got some suggestions from the people that work there and everyone that worked there recommended I should get a Fender Telecaster. They showed me a really cheap one and had a cool design so I got it.

A few of my favorite bands to play are... Papa Roach, System of a Down and Avenged Sevenfold (A7X). Papa Roach and System songs have good guitar rhythms, but not many solos. A7X is fun to play because they have a solo in every song and they're fun to learn and play. Papa Roach and System are somewhat similar but A7X is way different. I've learned around 4 of their songs, but only half of the whole song because it got difficult. Their guitarist, Synyster Gates, is amazing. I'll probably learn more of their music in a few years when I'm better at playing.

Since the time I got my 2nd guitar I've wanted to play and learn a lot more songs and techniques. I've gotten a ton better at playing just because I've practiced everyday for an hour or more. I used to hate practicing but now it's really fun since I know how to do stuff on it. Guitar has probably changed my life now.

How I Got Stitches
By George Papp

This is the story of how I busted open my elbow. It was last year in the ending of the school year. I had just got back from karate and I felt like skate boarding. I went inside to get my board and my mom told me to do my homework. I said "I'll do it in a little bit". So I went in my backyard and cleared off a big spot of blacktop. I got on my skate board and tried to do a kick flip and fell. When I was falling all I could think about is not breaking anything. Sure enough I forgot to move a thick sheet of steel. My elbow went strait into it. I got up and I brushed my self off and look on my arm and there was a gouge about two inches wide and one inch deep.

I walked inside casually while my arm was dripping blood, and asked my mom to look at it and she screamed "what the BEEP did you do!" I told her I was skate boarding and fell. I took a shower and got dressed. Then my mom drove me to the hospital. I had my blood pressure taken then the tried to give me a shot. I am so unbelievably afraid of needles! After I got over the fact that they were going to stick me I let the doctor give me numbing he threaded the needle.

All I was thinking about is I should have done my homework instead. After seven stitches he let me sit up and I left with my mom. On the way home she kept on saying "I told you, you should've done your homework. When I got home I still had to do homework. And from that day on when my mom told me to do something I usually do it. And from that day on when my mom told me to do something I usually do it.

Ride
by Chris Pecar

I really like to skateboard

But sometimes I can't afford the board's I like to ride

At least the kind that I need to ride

If you were to ride what kind would you like to ride there is to much to decide?

Sometimes I can't find what I like to ride

So it makes me want to find what I like to ride

When I find it I'm happy and kind

If you want to ride don't be shy people are kind

Go to the store and look for what kind you would like to ride

Once you do happen to find your kind

Then you need your trucks and your wheels

Then your done it's time to shine

Find a hill

Get ready get set and go

Careful or you're guaranteed to fall

If you do a good thing to know is 911 just make the call

Basketball

By: Lindsay Postal

Running down the court at full speed.
The game is tied. It's up to you.
Your heart is pumping, you must succeed!
You can't miss your lay-up,
Your team needs the lead.

You think about failure as you go.
Pressure?
More than you know!
What if you fall?
The crowd would scream "whoa!"

Your team could lose it all!
No, you shoot, you score.
You hear your coach call,
Above the crowd's screams,
"That's why we play basketball!"

My Brother's Messy Room
By Dillon Raymond

The destruction of a monsoon,
a step up from my brothers room .
there's no spot you can see the floor,
dirty laundry is his décor.
The floor boards swallowed his bed,
I know the cat is dead.
There's a jungle in his messy closet,
There's a lion in my net.`
Don't try to clean it you'll get stuck,
there`s tons and tons of muck.
trust me its not easy to ignore,
we find it hard to shut the door.

Lacrosse

By: Hailee Reimer

Under my skin are my muscles
    They allow me to
    run
    work hard,
    move my body,
    are united to my bones.
Under my muscles are my bones,
    They allow me to
    stand taller,
    be healthier,
    support my various organs,
    produce my red and white blood cells.
Under my bones is my heart,
responsible for pumping MY blood throughout MY body. All in all,
    It holds my love for lacrosse.
        The astonishing game I will never forget.
            The rush.
            Wind wafting in your hair,
            girl defending you gets to the ball before me,
            the twinge of pain.
            The swelling of my knee,
            pounding of my heart telling me to slow down,
            before it bursts
            knowing you can't stop.
            No matter what you can't let your guard down
            the ball is your number one goal never let it out
            of your sight
            the urge to make a goal.
            Catch the ball, 3 passes, every minute, should or
            shouldn't
            go for it, arms up, head echoing, shoot it, shoot it
            The compelling force of your arms to scoop the
            ball.
            You want to be the center of attention so charge
            towards the ball

get into position right knuckles touching ground,
knees bent
All no matter what.
Under my skin are my muscles, my bones, my heart, and my soul
all for lacrosse.

Cancer
By Isaiah Robles

In 2009, my friend Brandon's mom had cancer. She'd had it for eight years. Depressed and frightened for herself and her children she wondered when her time was going to come, when she would go to that special place. It had to be hard wondering where her son Brandon and her daughter Megan were going to go if she did pass or if she could overcome this horrible nightmare? Brandon was a kid that liked to do bad stuff like getting suspended, stealing and skipping school Because his mom had cancer he didn't know what to do with himself. He ended up in trouble!

Megan was a strong Individual. She did great in school, not just for herself but for mother and her family. One day she hoped to take care of her family so they wouldn't have to struggle so much. Brandon's mother was also strong, trying to overcome. She would sit at home all alone watching TV and smoking cigarettes. She tried enjoying her life while she could, living a day at a time, she prayed and wished that she could over come this nightmare.

Brandon's mother died on the day before Brandon's birthday. Brandon was so sad that he knew that his mother wouldn't be there for his 13th birthday. In the end, his mom is resting heaven, peaceful and happy, no more fear of death. Now she can watch over Brandon and Megan heads.

I don't know what it's like to lose a mom. I know it had to be very hard for Brandon and Megan. I don't know where they are now, but I hope they're all okay and in a great home with someone that cares about them, and teaches them to do the right thing. I also hope that Brandon makes good decisions in life. One day I'd like to run into him again. I would be so happy if I see him!

This is the Most Redundant Thing Ever
By: Kassi Rodriguez

Cleaning my bedroom.
Clothes in piles everywhere.
Old books dispersed around me.
All different kinds of shoes scattered up and down the closet.
Cleaning and cleaning, again and again.
What's the point in doing it all?
How do you describe cleaning?
Horrible, pointless, and boring.
Three very simple words to describe why I hate cleaning.
Who really cares?!
Not me. Not you. Oh yeah, my mother.
She's always yelling at me to get it done already.
Why should she care?
It's mine, and only mine.
I hate, hate, hate cleaning!!!
Can't you tell?

One Little Teardrop
By: Spencer Russell

Have you ever lost someone real close to you? Well, it hurts! Not just on the outside, it hurts on the inside too. If you ever experience it, you'll know how I feel. The pain from losing someone you love stabs your heart forever.

It was a couple years ago, when I lost a dear friend, Teardrop, my cat. He had large, trusting, green eyes shaped like teardrops, that's how he got his name. I can still picture them now. He was an extremely shy cat, you hardly ever saw him. He usually hid under the dining room table and big soft couches. But, he also loved to play. Occasionally he came out from hiding and bounced off walls trying to catch beaming red laser lights. He slobbered and chewed on string, and played with his loving brother, Gray. Teardrop's life couldn't have been any better.

Unfortunately, we started to notice odd behavior from him. He couldn't speak, couldn't move, he could barely even eat. We had to gently start lifting him up since he wasn't able to move on his own. We had to set him down at his food dish, just so he would eat. We tried to lay him in bed to get him to sleep, in hopes the he would get better. He couldn't do anything a cat typically did anymore. It was awfully depressing to hear him cry for help, when it seemed like no one was listening. I was asking myself "Is he going to live, or is he going to die?" Questions I couldn't answer.

Then on one tragic day, we made the decision to take him to a vet. That is when we found out he was suffering from cancer. My Teardrop was terminally ill!

I remember deciding to go with my mom to have Teardrop put down in peace. I wanted to have a chance to see him one last time. It was incredibly hard for me to see him suffer on my lap all the way to the vets. I felt terribly sick to my stomach. I wondered what everyone's reaction would be like when we came back home with no Teardrop.

The drive seemed like hours while we searched around to look for a good, proper place for Teardrop. Every vet was either closed or not for cats. Finally, after a long drive, we found one that would take Teardrop's pain away for good, and out of his misery.

****

We started heading for the building, and walked up to the counter. Immediately the veterinarian came to help. We told her what we needed, and she took us to this special room. I felt very queasy. As she and my mom were chatting, I could not take my eyes off of Teardrop. It was like we were communicating telepathically. Tears were rolling down my cheeks. Finally, I looked up and there was the nice lady staring at me, and she smiled. It was a very heartwarming grin that made me want to smile too, but I was too miserable to move my face at all.

That day was the last time I ever saw Teardrop. I gave him one last cherished hug, and then the veterinarian took him away. I never saw Teardrop again. I couldn't explain my feelings. Except that I was hurt deep down, way deep down, deeper than the deepest trench in the big ocean. I was devastated by the thought of him no longer being around.

On our drive home, my mom and I were still and calm. We had stopped crying and just stared out the window at the world around us. It was really strange, all our tears just suddenly dried up. I wonder why? I asked my mom, and she said it was because we knew Teardrop wasn't in pain anymore. I thought about that for a second, and knew that it was true and I was very glad about that.

It is somehow comforting to think that things are just meant to be in life. No matter how much it hurts as long as you have memories of your loved one, their heart will always be here with you. Teardrop is in a better place somewhere, and much happier than he was on Earth, and I'm ok with that!

What is Soccer?

By: Taylor Schantz

Soccer is a lifestyle,
One you can not quit.
Soccer is forever,
You just have to commit.

Soccer is a fun sport,
Whether you play for a team or not.
Soccer takes a lot of skill,
Like throwing down moves on the spot.

Soccer is the greatest,
And is being played worldwide.
Soccer gets crazy,
Whenever the game is tied.

Soccer is about leadership,
Like me being in charge.
Soccer is about teamwork,
Like working in a group that's large.

Soccer is about many things,
Like speed and determination.
Soccer is a lot of work,
And requires some preparation.

Soccer is a great sport,
Like football, baseball, or cheerleading.
Soccer is very physical,
With lots of bruises, scars, and bleeding.

Soccer is everywhere,
Like schools, TVs, and books.
Soccer has many uniforms,
But its not about the looks.

Runnin' Into the Unknown
By Caroline Schlaufman

We is crouched in the woods of Mississippi.
Me, nine – Mama and my sister, Jess.
Tryin' to get away from the evil they call slavery.
This is jus how it be in 1831.

We's push through the brush,
A dog barked, we froze.
It was the slave catchers!
I hide just me and Jess, without Mama.

I heared a scream.
Mama had been taken from us.
One bark o' a dog, and she was gone.
All we's had left was an echo that was dyin' fast.

I need to be brave;
I gotten through so much.
Without Mama I lost
I gots no hope.

Then a cry from the bundle in my arms,
Reminds me I have to keep goin' –
Not fer me,
Fer Jess.

Is there any water here?
I can see a river in the distance.
We's pushin' through the brush
Hopin' for food ahead.

I bring the hot, murky water to my lips;
We's spit out the bugs left in the water.
Mosquitos surround us
This here is all we have.

How does I provide for Jess?

She look sick.
How does ya know if a baby sick?
Mama woulda known what to do.

I don't know what to do.
I sits and cries,
So much to think of,
I need someone, someone bigger.

God, I say, ya my only hope
I need your guidance
We's need a glimmer of hope.
There ain't nothin' left.

I feel arms holdin' me.
Am I dyin', I think?
Is it all ova?
Peace at last?

No!
It a fellow runna-
He say his name is Moses
His arms are strong and true.

He has water and food,
I have no words for thankin'.
I feel a bit of that hope comin' back.
Although I feel no joy it has come soon.

Moses say Mama sent him.
Is Mama okay? I ask.
The look on his face,
I know, she gone.

I can't speak.
The only person I love;
Gone,
In the blink of an eye

I cry. My heart achin'
Moses put his arm around me.

I stay there for what seems like forever,
Then I let go.

I give him Jess,
He takes her with gentleness
She stirs and goes back to sleep,
A tiny smile on her face.

How can she be so happy?
She has no clue.
No father,
And now no memory of her loving mother.

The sadness is overwhelming,
But the night is comin.'
Moses say we can't stay here forever,
I wish we could.

At dusk I sigh,
It time to move on.
We head towards freedom,
I want to go back, but we's can't.

I trip and fall,
My ankle snaps.
Is it supposed to be that big?
I need somethin' cool.

I can't walk. Moses carry me the whole day,
He tell me I gonna be okay.
It still hurt though.

Then afta a long day,
We's see a house in the distance.
I know it safe!
Moses say not to get my hopes up.

But, it is!
Moses tell me we knows by the candles now.
I love candles now.
It is still risky though.

We's go into the house'
A nice lady come ova.
Jess cries,
This lady takes her.

"Oh, this po chil" she say,
"Did ya all have water for this chil?"
I reply that we's were stuck,
In the woods for two days.

She then ushers us in a closed room.
She say it's goin' be okay.
She hands us food and water.
She say that's all she have though.

I don't care if that's all.
We's have food and clean water;
The chicken is hot and crispy.
Moses say he will watch it.

The next day we leave,
Anotha safe house close by.
I think we's in Tennessee,
That's what Moses say.

We's hear a knock on the door,
It is time to move on.
We's been to so many of these things
I suppose to be in Pennsylvania soon.

We's see sign,
Moses say it the "Mason Dixon Line"
I don' care what it is
I free!

Moses he carry me fer hours.
He set me down and collapses
I feel like a burden,
How can I eva pay him back?

Moses take me by the hand,
I hobble along,
He put his arm around my shoulder
Moses keep me goin'.

I owe this person;
I hardly know,
Everythin'
He bend down and hug me tight.

We's reach a safe house.
Afta all this work,
We's safe!
I know it's okay.

I finally feel secure -
Moses is sittin' with Jess in his lap,
I know God sent this man –
Moses by name, angel in character.

Cherry Red Dodge
By: Jacob Sharrard

Here we go.
Vrooooooom!
Roars my engine.
Geez, can't you take it easy on me?

Owe, that burns!
But, it sounds really cool.
Ooh, my cherry red paint is really sparkling today.
Thanks, Sun!

Yo, dude chill!
Can you cool down a little bit?
You're going to make me overheat!
Oh no, I need an oil change.

I'm going to need some gas soon too.
Oh great, it's starting to rain,
Can't we go home?
This rain is going to make me rust!

Ahh, we're home!
Ooh, that towel feels good on my paint.
Finally, I'm dry. Now, I won't rust.
The rain stopped.

Here we go again.
Vrooooom.
Roars my engine.
Off we go.

High School
By Jason Short-Hibberd

High School is a whole new experience,
with brand new classes that make an appearance,
Chemistry, and Rocket Science, and Algebra II,
so many classes I can't even count,
have some patience there are a lot of choices.

High school is a brand new place,
with whole new people to meet and face.
Many different kinds of students
like sophomores, juniors and tons of seniors!
It makes a variety that I'm fine with.

High School isn't tough,
just don't fail and that'll be enough.
So, get great grades,
because it's a delight,
all of this to make your life right!

High school is the place to be,
just take constant lectures away from me.
All they do is rant and rave
I don't like those kinds of lessons,
make them go away!

Speed Demon
By Amber Slagle

Geez! It's hot out here; the sun is beating on my hood. Either we get this race on or put me back in the garage. Oh my gosh, do you see that black ugly race car over there parked at his trailer? Well, he is going down! We need to win this race – that black car needs to stop winning! He needs to give us a chance for once. Now, where is that Speed Racer? Finally, there she is! It's about time! Now, don't hurt me when you climb in. Hurry, get those belts on, put on the steering wheel and I will be ready! Here we go – burn rubber on that track!

I hate just sitting here and waiting for the race to start. I can only hold onto this energy for so long. We are starting just three places behind that black car. I know we can get him! I have been holding all this energy in all day and now I need to get rid of it! I think we might have a chance at winning this race. Now it's time to get that black car up there. He is just a couple of cars in front of us; he should be easy to catch. I told you we would beat him at least one time and I was not going to lie to my Speed Racer! So, let's go do this – he is going down! We are getting close just three laps to go and we are fourth. I still have a lot of energy Speed Racer let's get it together and put the gas to the floor. Yes, we are second! Oh no, green and white checkered and that black car is just right in front of us!

Now the race is over and we got second. The black car won again. I'm sorry Speed Racer, we will get him next time – I promise you that! Now look at my car it is so beat up, but that is okay. I will be all fixed up and happy again. But look at it this way, it is part of racing. Time to be put in the trailer. Now I'm in the trailer all strapped down and we should be on our way home very soon. We are on our way home and as the trailer goes over bumps, I bounce and my shocks go up and down. Finally, we are home. Speed Racer put me back in the garage until the next race. Now I am all sleepy and I think it is time for me to get going to bed. Good night.

By Colin Smith

-Modern Warfare 2-
RPG's and Rifles,
Repeaters and knives.
Blood so hot,
Marines taking lives.
Ducking and firing.
Making more gore.
Guns, Guns,
This makes War.

-Metroid Prime 3-
Beams and Rockets,
Pirates and Marines.
Face covered with sweat,
Samus fighting Machines.
Shooting and rolling.
Facing more eruption.
Phazon, Phazon,
This makes corruption.

-Xbox 360-
Controllers and Remotes,
Systems White or Black.
Graphics so cool,
Just like a Mac.
Live or Local,
Making some Friends.
Battles, Battles,
This Game Ends

-Wii-
Wiimotes and Nunchucks,
Sensors and Motion.
Controls so Good,
Causing a Commotion.
Miis in Games,
Wi-Fi Races,
Wii Wheel, Wii Wheel,
Take some paces.

Runt
By: Rachel Sondergeld

Wow it's great on this new farm, I know I just got here a couple weeks ago but I already love the place the only problem is that golf cart riding do, oh and that golf carts scary too. Oh no here it comes "no go away golf cart". "What scared of a little golf cart Runt", "Your just as small as me Pup you're a wiener dog and I'm a baby pig." "Yeah but your afraid of a golf cart" "No I'm not" "really, then get on it right now" "fine I will"!

Wow that wasn't as scary as I thought it would be. "Ah now all I have to do is get situated". "Ah what's happening" "your laying on the gas pedal you idiot, get up", "I can't, my foot is jammed under the pedal". "Hurry we're headed strait for that orange tree". I'm so scared the weeded long grass is rushing around me we're getting farther away from the house, and in the barn I can hear the chickens clucking and the pigs snorting, no one knows what to do, I can still smell the scent of the fresh country air but it's not comforting like before, right now it just reminds me of how bad I screwed up. "Look Aunt Alice, look she's running after us" "Yeah too bad there's no way she'll catch us". "Try and get your foot unstuck" "I can't it's twisted around and getting smashed by my own body weight, there's no way I can get up" "Can you try to reach the gas petal I can't push it down on my own" "I'm trying but I can't reach over to it".

"Can't those people up there on the seat do anything"; "I don't know their panicking too". "Why did that one just jump off"? "We are flying toward an orange tree at high speed, your stuck on the gas petal we're most likely going to crash, why wouldn't she jump off" "The driver could still save us" "that's comforting since she's only been driving for a day" "you didn't have to come on the golf cart with me" "Whoa what just happened, why did the cart jolt" "She hit the brake, we're saved, what's wrong" "We were lucky, you could have killed us" "But wait, come on it's not my fault". "Yeah I know, it was an accident, but I also know that Aunt Alice is going to kill us". His laugh was raspy and different I didn't even know dogs could laugh."Hey can I ask you something" "What is it Runt" "Are we friends now Pup" "yeah I guess we are" "Get back here Runt, you too Pup, animals these days".

Basketball Brings Out My Family
By: Noah Stinson

Basketball is indescribable. My dad introduced me to the game when I was about 4 years old and I've loved it ever since. It is so incredible because you can be very creative depending on how you play it. Like my brother who taught me all the fancy stuff I like to do. How to dribble with my knees, pass around my back and do trick shots like no other, like my famous shot behind the backboard that I love to do because I make it all the time. He taught me how to really have fun with basketball. I work on my game every day by going in the driveway to practice my shooting and dribbling that I need to be a good point guard. I also try to never miss practices so that I can work on all the fundamentals that I have to have to be a great player.

My dad coached the teams all the way through elementary. He always knew when to pull a player, or come up with a good play when the game was close. My dad takes me to the gym just so I can practice shooting and fundamentals. He puts a lot of effort into basketball and I can never thank him enough. As a kid during the spring and summer, I would always go to my sisters' basketball tournaments. The only reason I went was so that I could shoot during their timeouts and halftimes. I still go to their tourneys today, but now I really watch how they play and see how I can evolve their great defense, boxing out and scoring ability into my basketball skills. My mom is that lady who is always yelling at the referees about a bad call, but she comes to most of my games cheering for me and supports me even when I'm not doing well. I love my family and I would never be playing basketball today if it wasn't for them.

I played in 3rd grade for my very first team, the Riverside Racers. I played center and power forward for Riverside because I was one of the tallest players on the team. We never loss a single game in elementary and that carried on to 6th grade were our Pierce team went undefeated also. Sixth grade was a really fun basketball season because we killed every team we played by at least 20 points because of the talent we had. Seventh and eighth grade is where it got serious. We were fighting to be the first undefeated boys basketball team in Pierce middle school history and it's the first season that we got competition! I made the pierce basketball team both seventh and eighth grade years. In 7th grade we went 7-3 overall, which was a winning record. In 8th grade we did slightly better by going 8-2 but we should have won the games we lost due to bad refereeing, missed lay-ups and missed free throws. Those seasons were really fun and exciting for getting the feel of competition for the first time.

I can't live without basketball and I can't live with my family without basketball in our lives. Basketball brings out the best in me and my family especially when we're all out on the court playing together. I am going to play basketball as long as I live no matter what my condition is. It is my passion and I'm sure it's my family's too. I love basketball but I love my family even more, it's such a great experience to have supporting role models around you at something you love. I can't thank my family enough for being there for me when I need it the most.

The Bracket
By: Patrick Stoddard

Yeah that's right I'm a College Basketball March madness bracket. Anyone has a problem with that.......... Okay then lets move on. Yeah. Being a Bracket is a pretty tough life. You get written on, spilled on, and even ripped to shreds. Oh and your life expectancy is normally March 1st- March 31st. Then we get torn up or ripped, if the humans have a bad bracket. But we could live longer if the humans have a good bracket, we will get shown off, or even bragged about. Then when we do get thrown away we brag about it to the other brackets in the trash fill. I mean sure, maybe I won't be the best bracket or even a winning won. I might not even be in one piece, when I get to the trash dump. But if you're a winning bracket your treated like a king whole or not.

But its not like the humans did much to make a bracket, we do all the hard work oh yeah picking up a pen or pencil is such hard work, and then they have to write 64 teams on us ohhh so much work. We get written on which actually hurts a lot, then the eraser hurts even more. Also come on who would have Kansas, Syracuse, or Kentucky going all the way it will obviously be Duke. But the human child that made me has Kansas winning it all. I think his name is Patrick and he is not really that bright, he bumps into walls for no reason, and hits his head a lot. But he's not doing so well this year so I fear I might be ripped. But I've tried to tell him several times to change his bracket but he just wont do it I don't even know if he can speak brakish, or even if he is deaf. But I could be like a basketball god or a guru.

I mean were like slaves we get punished for things we didn't even do, and we can't even speak up because apparently the humans can't understand us. I mean humans are supposed to be the most advanced and smartest creatures on earth but come on they can't even guess who's going to win a college basketball championship out of 64 teams. So I not sure about them being the smartest race on earth but at least they made paper so that's a start. Oh crap, here comes the human boy. He looks mad, because Duke just won and he hates Duke, oops he bumped in to another wall, hahahahahahahah! Wait he just picked me up oh no he's ripping me ahhhhhhhhhhhhhhhhhhhhhhhhhh! Please, no not that trash anything but the trash. NO! NO! NO!

As I lay in a bad smelling trash bag with a lot of trash, I realized being a bracket really sucks! I wish I could have been a menu at Big Boys like my brothers, at least then you only get spilled on, drooled on, and as a bonus you get to live for like a year or so. I was just laying there thinking I hate being a bracket, when the big human male, who is like an alpha bracket (the leader of the pack). Opened the lid and threw a huge bag on top of me, then picked me and the bag I as in up, which slid more foul smelling items on me then threw me in a huge can like thing that smelled worse then the bag, and had disgusting bugs roaming the can. I hate being a bracket.

Biking
By Frankie Skrelja

Biking is so sweet,
B ut it can knock you off your feet.
Be careful when you go hit the rail,
You could get scared and bail.

When you hit a jump,
You usually land on a lump.
When you go off a stair,
You get lost of air!

If your foot slips off the pedal,
You skin might hit metal.
Biking is really fun,
You can get tan in the sun.
When you fall it's kind of rough,
But you got to be tough.
Biking takes lots of skill,
You also got to have the will.
Biking can make you a star,
You got to push your self to see who you are…

My Dog
By Joe Stonehouse

My dog is the best dog in the world. He is very dumb all the time but I love my dog, even when he makes me really mad. His name is Jackson (I didn't name him), he is a big black Labrador. He loves to go in my trash because he loves food. He is a fat little dog. I'm his favorite of all in my family. He sleeps on the couch in my room and snores really loud and wakes me up in the middle of the night when he dreams about the mailman.

He hates when I flick his nose because he sneezes about five times after I flick his nose. His favorite food is butter; he ate a whole stick of butter in five seconds before, without taking a single bite of it. He loves walks and car rides, whenever I leave for hockey I look out my window pulling out of the driveway and I can see him laying on top of the den couch and waits for us to come back. My dog thinks he is a cat because he will always jump on the very top part of the couch and lay on my head, but he only stays there for a little bit and he is so fat he falls off. He also thinks he is a cat because, I swear, I heard him meow before! He also has tried to jump on my counter like my old cat, but he never makes it up there, he just knocks down a bunch of plates and glasses and starts to whine.

My dog likes to make a mess and make people mad. He loves to take stuff out of the garbage and rip it to pieces in the living room in front of my dad just to make him mad. When my dad gets up to grab it Jackson runs into my room and rips the rest of the object on my couch, which after I have to clean up the mess.

My dog is super strong. When we take him on walks he takes us for a walk instead. When I try to take him for a walk, he tries to chase down passing cars, but never realizes that he can't catch them. Jackson is also very clever. One time when I went to take off his shock collar and I was on my rollerblades, he pulled me out of my driveway. His shock collar was in my hand stuck between the leash and my hand and it zapped me for about a minute! I definitely saw him smile.

My dog reminds me of Marley from <u>Marley and Me</u> because when we try to take him on car rides he will try to jump out the window. We can only crack the window and whenever it is cracked a little more, he sticks his head out the window and then his paws go out of the car. At that point he thinks he can fit his entire body out the window, but he can't because he is a little over weight. I think Jackson thinks the air is food because when he tries to jump out the window he stops and then opens his mouth and bites the air. Occasionally he will catch a bug in his mouth and throw up out the window.

Jackson has broken a lot of stuff like my bike tire, my favorite stuffed animal when I was six, my mom's paint job on her car, my television, a lot of X-Box games have been mysteriously disappearing and then reappearing in the morning with big scratches and cracks on them. He also broke my giant Lego city I built when I was nine. He was really hyper one day and grabbed my favorite (second favorite) stuffed animal from a long time ago. He bolted out the door, down the hall and busted the door into my storage room. He jumped and rolled all over my big Lego city and completely destroyed it.

My dog is sometimes (most of the time) annoying. He is sometimes really calm and lazy when we get back from running or the park because he is so tired. He doesn't even get a drink of water, he falls asleep at the end of my bed and cuts the circulation off of my legs, and bites my feet in his sleep. But, he is my dog and he is here to stay. (Yay!)

The Divorce
By Chase Swartwood

Dad, I remember when you and mom were still married, and how happy our family was when we were all together. Now that you're divorced I feel that our family is just falling apart. We barely had a start. I mean Ashton and I were so little, only six and mom was a big part of my life. The divorce was very hard on us. Mom has a new boyfriend, Brian, but it's not the same at all. I wish you were still together. Even with Karma, (yea, it's fun when she's over) it's just not the same at all.

I'm writing this just to let you know how much I care about our family. Hopefully nothing else bad happens, because I can't take anymore of this! Why did you have to get a divorce? Every time I ask you, you just ignore me and act like I'm not even there. When you got divorced did you even think about me or Ashton and how much this would affect us? Please give me a real reason why you got a divorce so I can accept it and not be sad and depressed about it.

Mom, I know that you're still good friends with dad. Why can't you tell Brian that? He knows that you talk still, and your still friends. Mom, I think you should tell Brian that you're still friends. He can get over that you have guy friends. He hangs out with his friends a lot, so you can do the same. I think that you should lay down the law with him! Tell him he can't do whatever he wants while you sit at home waiting for him. But, if you didn't get divorced in the first place you wouldn't have had to deal with Brian.

So mom and dad, can you please just tell me and Ashton why you got divorced? Why did you divorce in the first place? You talk on the phone everyday and talk to each other a lot, you act like really good friends and all that. I wish you just would have told me why you got divorce and I'll be happy and get over everything! Unfortunately I doubt that will ever happen. But until that day I will just have to live my life one day at a time until it gets better.

Slowly, my life is getting better. I'm getting more used to it now. It doesn't make me as sad when I can't see my mom or dad. I do see my mom way more than I used to, and for longer too. I get to see her for three to four hours every couple days. I guess I can deal with it just the way it is right now, at least, for a little while longer.

No Longer Mine

By: Ruby Vailliencourt

Do you know how bad it hurts,
when I see you go and the pain gets worse?
Do you know how hard it is to hold back tears,
and run away from all the fears?
I know you don't care,
why did you make me think that way?

You thought you could pull me in and then disappear?
Well this is what you need to hear:
You broke my heart,
I know it sounds so cliché,
but you were the one that made me sing,
the one I thought would heal everything.

All the feelings never fade,
you never let me feel betrayed.
Laying there with you,
wrapped in your arms forever.
But no- my fantasy has to end,
because you reveal this was all just pretend.

You messed with my head,
you made me come undone,
all because I thought you were the one.
You knew you were playing around,
and finally, I found a flaw in you.
Why didn't I get the clue?

So all the perfect things,
I have to leave behind,
like my peace of mind,
it took me so long to find,
because you just revealed,
you are no longer mine.

By: Sabrina Vue

Love…
    Starts as friendships,
    Honest,
    Fair,
    And trusting
Moving towards acquaintances…
    Hugs,
    Kindness,
    And closeness,
    Good-hearted…
That becomes love…
    Holding hands,
    Joy,
    Blissfulness…
That lasts forever
    Content…
    Your one and only…
    The mate who's open and deep…
    True love…
That closeness we had was
Unforgettable, so when
I'm lonely…I'll come and find you.

deep, mindful, and openhearted.
Acquaintances
hugs, kindness, and closeness…
a mate, who's open and deep.
Love
committed, good-hearted, and your one and only.
Forever
holding hands…
blissfulness…
content and joy…
and
embracing.
That closeness we had was unforgettable, so when

145

I'm lonely.... I'll come and find you.

Love is everywhere
It fills up sweet smelling air.
Love is happiness.
It means a lot when you're sad.
They help you up, and tear you down.
They're there forever.
As you're life goes on,
You'll always remember the comfort of them.
    When you look at me, I smile.
    When you hug me, I feel loved.
    When you hold my hand, I feel alive inside.
    When you're by my side, I feel precious.
    When we are together, you complete me.
Sorry is just a word, coming out of your mouth.
You never meant it.
Your love for me is just a play.
The love you gave was fake.
Everything we did is an unforgettable memory, to me.
Your love was everything.
You made me feel beautiful.
But your love was fake.
Not mine....
    Love means being together forever,

I Will Be There

By Anonymous

My sister, Katie got diagnosed with type 2 diabetes in 2002. In type 2 diabetes, either the body does not produce enough insulin or the cells ignore the insulin. She has to check her blood sugar and give herself insulin shots every day until they find a cure, which is probably going to be a long time. Every day I worry about her. She has to make sure her blood sugar is not too high or too low, it has to be just right. If it's not, then she could go into a seizure.

I remember one day that my family and I were home. We heard a "THUMP" upstairs. We rushed to where we heard the thump, and we found my sister just lying on the floor shaking. The next thing I heard was my mom yelling at my dad, "MARK, MARK! CALL 911!!! HURRY!!!"

I didn't know what to do…just sat there and watched. My mom yelled and told me to get the glucose (sugar) so she can put it in Katie's mouth to get her blood sugar up and hopefully it could help Katie to get out of the seizure. So I got the glucose, my mom went to go put it in Katie's mouth, next thing I knew, Katie bit my mom's finger! I was nervous. I could hear the ambulance rushing outside the window. I still didn't know what to do, so I just went upstairs to my room and started crying. Paramedics arrived. I didn't know what they were going to do because I was upstairs just balling my eyes out. My dad came upstairs to tell me that my sister and my mom were taken to the hospital. Apparently, Katie bit my mom's finger so hard, that my mom has to get treated too. I will never forget that day.

In 5th grade, there was another terrible day. All of my friends and I were obsessed with these electronic 'Tamagotchi' toys. We weren't allowed to have them in class, but it didn't matter to me. I was playing with mine and my 5th grade teacher, Mr. Kochevar, caught me and took it away. I was really nervous of what my mom would say. Would she get mad? Will she yell at me? Will I get grounded? I hope not. I got into my mom's car after school. I told my mom that I got the toy token away, but she didn't listen. She was too busy on the phone screaming, "OKAY, I'LL BE RIGHT THERE!!!" I didn't know what was going on.

We got to Kettering High School and I saw paramedics rushing into the building. I hoped they weren't for my sister, but they were. I ran in seeing my sister on the ground with paramedics around her. I tried to hold back the tears, but it didn't work. My mom told me the story after the paramedics left. My sister was at poms practice, and her blood sugar was running low, so she broke into a seizure. When she hit the floor, some of her bottom teeth fell out. When she went to the hospital, some paramedics were still at Kettering looking for her teeth. They found them and the dentist pushed them into Katie's gum at the hospital. That day, I will never forget.

Now, in present day, she doesn't have seizures as often as she used too. Now I know what to do when my sister's blood sugar runs low. Throughout the hard times that my sister had, I will always love her, care about her, and I will always be there for her.

My Sister

By Katlyn Wasnich 4th hour

Does she know how much I care about her? Does she know how much I love her? Does she even know that I miss her? I always remember asking my dad, "Daddy, when is Sarah coming home?"

It would be awhile before I would really get to see her. She lives in Georgia. I don't know where in Georgia but, she's there. She's in college, but really young for a college student. She's nineteen, but she started college at age sixteen because she was home schooled and never had summer. So she had school all year and it moved her up faster. Sarah is my step sister. She is my dad's daughter. My dad got divorced from her mom and then he married my mom. Together they had Matt, Andrew, and I.

Every time Sarah came to Michigan to visit, my dad would tell me that she was coming home and staying for a long time. I would get so excited and my heart would race. We would go do activities. Once we went bowling and then putt-putting. I remember after two days, I walked in my bedroom, (that Sarah I were sharing) and she was packing up. I kept asking why are you getting your stuff together? She just ignored me. Eventually she told me that she was going back to Georgia. I remember how sad I was and I ran out to my play set in the backyard. I cried and cried for hours. It was four years until I got to see her the next time.

I don't really know her as well as I want to. Every time I see her she's a new person. Last time I saw her, she was drawing pictures for comic books, and she was amazing at drawing! I love her personality too. I love how she colors her hair all these different colors and she doesn't care what people think of it. I remember seeing her with blue then green then pink highlights, it looked so cool. One day, Sarah and I went out and got some wash out hair die and colored my hair red! It didn't work out that well, so I just got this machine that did highlights. I did washable blue hair and I loved it. Now she seems different, I don't know if she just is getting more mature or what, but she's not as fun and energetic as she used to be.

If Sarah were here I know we would be close. I would tell her everything about boys, my friend problems, and how I feel about everything in the world. I can't do that if she's not here with me. All I have is my brothers and they don't want to listen to girl problems. I mean what boys do? I would be able to share moments funny or even bad. I do try to talk to her when she is here but there is just too much to tell. I get to see her and that's all that matters.

As much as I want to see her all the time I can't. I get that she's in college and she wants to be with her mom in Georgia too. Maybe after college she will visit more and we could be there with each other through everything. I miss her like crazy, but she is still my sister and I love her.

What It Was
By: Kayla White

Friendship means…
    kindness and understanding,
    inside jokes and crazy pranks,
    constant company.
Friendship can also mean…
    hurtful words and blank stares,
    arguments and rumors,
    and shattered trust.
It can become…
    shy smiles and injured eyes,
    awkward hello's and relieved goodbye's,
    eventual apologies.
We wish it could be…
    what it was before,
    but it never will be,
    because we can't remember,
    what friendship means.

FRIENDS
BY: CAMERON WISENBAUGH

Friends, they can be jerks, but most of the time their helpful. They can help you with your homework, or even help you do chores. Those chores can be anything, like, rake the leaves, wash a car, and maybe mow the lawn. Sometimes they would have to supply most of the equipment to do most of those chores. If they break anything they would have to pay for it, unless it's theirs.

My friends are popular, so that makes me popular. Some of them like to hang out, and most like to chill. Most of my friends like to play videogames. One of my friends likes to stay the night. Its time to go to bed, we just stay up all night and talk, and maybe play some videogames. One of my other friends likes to play outside, so he taught me how to climb a tree.

Some of my other friends like to hunt, so I have help from them to learn to shoot. Basically all of my friends back me up. If someone's messing with me they get in it, and back me up. If they are sad, or mad I cheer them up, if I'm sad, they do the same.

One of my friends really likes to ride my quad, so basically every day he asks me if he could ride it. When we ride, if we do so, we do it in the 200 and something foot long backyard of ours. We make tracks around the yard, so then maybe if we ride it for a long time, you could see the tracks around it? That friend always likes to either ride, or ride quads, or even play videogames. It's hard to figure out what he wants to do. Most friends are like that, but not all of them.

If I'm stuck on a homework assignment, they always help me out. If I don't get what to do on an assignment they teach me what to do. Even if I wasn't there the day before and I missed the assignment, they would tell me what to do. When I missed a day, and we had a lot of homework that day, on that day, they would tell me how much we got, and for what classes. When I got the assignments, I would ask them how to do it, what page it was on, and if it was math, I would ask them what equation we had to use for the problems.

Those are just how my friends are. They can be really cool, funny, and some times jerks, but hey, I can't complain. You will always have your ups and downs. Most of the time there is a lot of drama, witch you shouldn't have to deal with. But it's all a supposed to work out great. That's how friends are supposed to be!

Never Thought I'd Have to Go on Without You
By: Ricky Wood

On the fourteenth of October 2006,
my mother passed away.
Peaceful and waiting for this in her bed,
and finally the moment was here.

She knew it wouldn't be long now,
and made sure everyone else knew too.
The family waited in shock ,
no one knew how to prepare for this.

Then her eyes gently closed,
and her skin slowly turned pale and cold.
 We knew, she was finally free,
finally home, finally at peace.

As her body was laid into the casket,
there was only one thing to think…
She's up in the clouds looking down,
 with a big smile on that face.

Thankfully now all her pain has died too.
Now there's nothing to do but lie here,
 and think of how things could be.
I miss you mom!

The Alien
Mikayla Woodiwiss

Once upon a time there was a man and his family, they went out to look at the sky. Suddenly, they saw a flash of light. They thought it was a falling star. But it wasn't because as they watched it crashed in the forest. The man turned to his wife and said," I am going to check the forest."

"No!" his wife named Van Jam said. "It's too dangerous! It could have been an asteroid or an alien ship."

Shake Jam, their son replied, "Mom, Dad should go check it out and see what it is."

Finally Van said, "All right, let's go and see what it is, but don't be crying if you get blown up or killed!"

They saw two aliens and a spaceship. The hole in the earth was the same size and shape as the spaceship which was now propped up and the doors were opening. Two aliens came out the door. One was big and green with red eyes and it walked closer and closer to the family. The second alien followed closely behind.

The aliens stopped right in front of the family and the two aliens said, "Humans, we come in peace."

Van said, "That's what they all say!"

Shake hugged his little brother Sam and replied, "Why are you here?"

The largest of the two aliens answered. "Why? To take over the whole world, crush it out of existence, of course, and to take people back to our ship. We want to make you slaves and brainwash you.

The father stepped protectively in front of his family, "I won't let you take my family to become slaves or let you brainwash us! I will kill you if you try to take any people to your ship."

The aliens saw Bob's gun and became scared. They dashed back to the ship and left the planet, never to be seen again.

Six years later the man and his family lived happily. His kids grew up. Shake was married and Sam moved on to middle school. They never saw the aliens again.

The Black Eye
By Michael young

Finally another practice. Just sitting here with my baseball family .Up here we go the bucket's up, he must be putting us in the car. If you don't know yet I'm a baseball . life as a baseball is pretty cool you get visit lots of places or you sit in one spot for a while. Anyway I'm ready to go to practice, PLOP! That was a bump. I'm just sitting here in this blue bucket. Waiting, waiting yes finally I'm going to be thrown. The top was opening, wow. Look how bright it is outside this bucket.

Everyone look it's a hand. Pick me, pick me no not him me. Then the hand grabs me and I'm off. I was put in a glove and then I flow into another and another. That went on for a while then the hit.

We were just being hit and returned, hit and returned. Then the fat blue guy picks me. I was up off the ground and tossed in the air, and I'm hit.

I was flying then sinking. I hit the ground right before the second baseman. He caught the ball throw it to the first baseman. The first baseman was the fat blue guy's son. He caught me, stepped on first. For some reason he thought it was a good idea to throw it to third. But it was a terrible throw. Then I was spinning and spinning. It was like a scene from a movie. Then POP!, I hit someone the pitcher right in the the left eye. Oh no did I hurt him. He's on the ground .Go people go. He must be really hurt.

He's up off the ground he going to the benches. Holy cow look at that eye, he's a purple spot the size of me. Where did every body go, oh they all around the kid I hit.

Well about ten to 20 minutes later he went to the car and drove off in a rush. Then the fat guy came and pick up the balls and I was back in the blue bucket. And I just have to forget it until next practice, I can't wait.

If You Give a Monkey Peanut Butter
By Alexis Zinn

If you give a monkey peanut butter, he will ask for jelly and bread.
When he puts the jelly and peanut butter on the bread, he will want the crust cut off.
So you'll bring it to your older brother, and he will cut off the crust.
When you brink it back to the monkey, he will want it cut into squares.
So you will bring it back to your older brother and he will cut it into squares.
When you bring it back to the monkey, he will scarf it down.
When he is done eating, he will want a glass of milk.
So you'll bring the milk and a glass to your older sister, and she'll fill the glass with milk.
You'll bring it back to the monkey, and he will thirstily chug it down.
You'll put him in front of a mirror, and he will laugh at his milky mustache.
So he will lick it off, and then get a good idea.
So he will hand you art supplies, and ask you to make paper mustaches.
So you'll bring the supplies to your sister and brother, and they will make paper mustaches.
You will go to the monkey, and you'll both wear a mustache.
The monkey and you will laugh and play, but the monkey will get hungry soon.
So you will give him some peanut butter, and he will ask for jelly and bread.

The Tragedy
By Steffen Zoner

Everybody knows about the war against terrorism. People think that they know all about the war. They think that no one else knows what their talking about. Well do they know why it started? Do they know why the terrorist are mad at us? , Well I'm going to tell you these questions and the views of people that support and don't support the war.

Some people are for the war against terrorism and some people are against it. Most people are for the war because of all the bad things terrorists have done to the U.S. like 9/11 when they took the World Trade Center from the U.S. and the world. Also when they crashed the plain into the pentagon. But what really makes them mad is that all the attacks that U.S. citizens try to do. When they have lived in the U.S. most of their life.

Most people that agree with the war are true U.S. citizens. Most true U.S. citizens try to encourage younger people to join the military and get back at the terrorist's that have done so much to our country. They have ruined our economy, and a lot of other things.

People that disagree with it because they want world peace. They think we should stop because we started this war with the terrorists. They think it's our fault that they hate the U.S

This war is all about religious beliefs. They don't like that people from their country come here and believe what religion they want. They don't like that Muslim woman can just wear what they want and say what they want to there husbands. They really don't like that people say that their Muslim and they don't even pray to their god or celebrate any of the Holidays. The terrorist's are mostly Muslim. They think that the U.S. is trying to take over the world. That the U.S. controls the world and no one can stop us.

Some people think that all Muslims are bad people and want to destroy our country even more. The truth is that not every person you think that will harm our country will actually do it. A lot of them just want to come to America just to get away from all the war and dictators that happens else where. Not a lot of people understand that and they need to start to understand.